THE YOUNG FRONTIERSMAN Series - Book 5

FORTITUDE

The Frontiersman Returns

I0608428

Matthew Blaine

MILFORD HOUSE

an imprint of Sunbury Press, Inc.
Mechanicsburg, PA USA

MILFORD HOUSE

an imprint of Sunbury Press, Inc.
Mechanicsburg, PA USA

For information about special discounts for bulk purchases, please contact Sunbury Press Orders Dept. at (855) 338-8359 or orders@sunburypress.com.

To request one of our authors for speaking engagements or book signings, please contact Sunbury Press Publicity Dept. at publicity@sunburypress.com.

FIRST MILFORD HOUSE PRESS EDITION: March 2025

Set in Adobe Garamond Pro | Interior design by Crystal Devine | Cover by Lawrence Knorr | Edited by Katarina Rivera.

Publisher's Cataloging-in-Publication Data
Names: Blaine, Matthew, author.
Title: Fortitude : the frontiersman returns / Matthew Blaine.
Description: First trade paperback edition. | Mechanicsburg, PA : Milford House Press, 2025.
Summary: Old friends call on Barnabas Locke to thwart the theft of Ute gold by a secret French expedition. Loyalties are tested when his cousin arrives to intercept that gold for the new U.S. government. Ride along on a keelboat down the Ohio, a buffalo stampede, an earthquake, standoffs, escapes, and murders with a touch of romance in a story true to the West.
Identifiers: ISBN : 979-8-88819-299-3 (paperback).
Subjects: YOUNG ADULT FICTION / Action & Adventure / General | YOUNG ADULT FICTION / Historical / United States / Colonial & Revolutionary Periods | FICTION / Action & Adventure.

Designed in the USA
0 1 1 2 3 5 8 13 21 34 55

For the Love of Books!

To storytellers everywhere

CONTENTS

ACKNOWLEDGMENTS

I am grateful to Lawrence Knorr, Publisher of Sunbury Press, for his confidence in printing this sequel to "The Young Frontiersman" series. A number of my readers had asked me if there was another book in the offing, and I am grateful to them for their interest in following the adventures of Barnabas Locke and Squando, the Abenaki Prophet. I hope this book meets the expectations of both my publisher and my public (in other words, my friends, family and readers who enjoy a ripping good yarn).

A special word of thanks is again due to my first readers—the always insightful Jim and Denise Glenn and my brother Stephen Balchunas, who reads with the vigilant outdoorsman's experience. My sister Alane Balchunas provided invaluable computer skills to the enterprise.

INTRODUCTION

STORYTELLING plays an essential part in my preceding books entitled "The Young Frontiersman" series, as they do in this sequel. Telling stories, especially around campfires, was traditionally entertainment, education, and a perpetuation of oral history. Letters do appear in these books; several in *Fortitude: The Frontiersman Returns*, but in those days people of the frontier spread information chiefly through word of mouth. The Native Peoples of the Plains ingeniously invented a form of hand talk for easy communication among the differing tribes throughout the West.

The attentive reader may notice that distances and times are seldom given specifically in these pages. The distances are vast, but the time it took to cross those distances was highly individual, depending on the means of transport, the weather, and the unpredictable events that might occur along the way—a swollen river, a lost horseshoe, a sudden encounter. This storyteller prefers to allow stories to unfold in fictional time, where my characters are free to wander at will.

The inspiration for this story arose from legends that still stir gold fever in the mountains of Colorado.

In 1859, the boom began in mining for gold, silver, copper, and lead. Barnabas Locke and his Ute allies did their best to forestall this inevitable invasion of gold seekers, but all that the fictional Squando, the Abenaki Prophet, foresaw came to a sorry pass. This book is set during the last years when Native Peoples of the West still exercised autonomy over their lands and cultures and interacted with white traders to mutual advantage. This was before the Lewis and Clark Expedition of Discovery opened the floodgates to white expansionism.

Fortitude picks up the storylines of the preceding books while introducing new characters—fictional, historical, and legendary. Not all of the reader's questions of "What happened to . . ." will be answered. This story hinges on international greed for the potential riches of the American West before it was even in American hands. The Spanish, the French, the British, and the Americans all played significant roles in the burgeoning trade in buffalo hides, beaver pelts, and furs for an international market. The first hints of a vast subterranean wealth in gold, silver, and minerals hastened the conquest of the American continent. All of these competing interests are reflected in the entire series and most specifically in this sequel to "The Young Frontiersman" stories.

The earthquake that figures as a plot device in *Fortitude* was inspired by firsthand accounts of the four centered on New Madrid, Missouri, occurring from December 16, 1811, through February 7, 1812. They remain the strongest ever recorded east of the Rocky Mountains. The earth shook as far north as Canada.

I chanced upon an essay, entitled "How American Indian Storytelling Differs from the Western Narrative Structure," that appeared in the December 15, 2021, issue of the School Library Journal (SLJ). The author is Dan SaSuWeh Jones of the Ponca tribe, author of *Living Ghosts & Mischievous Monsters*. He describes how Native Americans do not tell stories the same way Europeans do. Native stories are nonlinear without plots or necessarily a beginning, middle and end. Many stories don't end at all and many characters who die in one story are lively in another. The story might start at the end or in the middle. It's an oral tradition in which Native Peoples hold rigidly to their beliefs about how stories and songs are told and passed down. Many stories are told in song with the accompaniment of a drum. "The story may be more about the journey than the resolution." Dan SaSuWeh Jones cites the excellent example of the classic Coyote stories of the Plains peoples' mythologies. These stories become more complicated and adult in content as the listener ages. In *Fortitude*, I mention the Winter Count—a tribe's record of its year of events painted in picture graphs on a buffalo robe.

Laid out in a nonlinear fashion, it is read from the center as the picture graphs spin out in a spiral. As I dedicate *Fortitude* to storytellers everywhere, it is important that the reader understands how differently stories can be told and interpreted.

I tried to capture the realism of the peoples I'm writing about, not as white or native, but as human beings living authentic lives. It is impossible for me to inhabit the skin and mind of peoples of widely different cultures living centuries ago, but I strongly believe that I can tap into the roots of shared humanity. This is a work of fiction, after all, not an ethnographic study. It is entertainment, a long story to be told around a campfire.

Matthew Blaine
Storyteller
January 2025

PROLOGUE

Late April of 1798 on the Plains

Five Frenchmen rode fast out of the mountains and onto the plains. After nearly twenty days on horseback, they were desperate to reach the trading post at the old French fort on the banks of the Missouri River. Each horse that collapsed from the relentless gallop or put a hoof into a prairie dog hole forced another horse to carry double weight until that horse collapsed in turn. The men had fled the carnage in the mountains with nothing to sustain them but their will to survive. The wounded died unburied. The survivors carved meat from the fallen horses and pressed on. Some uncounted days ago, they first noticed the trackers behind them. The Frenchman the trackers had marked as the strongest, the one most likely to reach the old fort alive, had raised a defiant fist and shaken it at the two distant figures.

The trackers, leading two packhorses, had no mercy in their hearts. The fleeing men had to die, but they preferred that the Frenchmen die of their wounds, of exposure, of exhaustion and hunger. But none could reach the safety of the old fort and reveal the secret of the mountains.

About a day's march from the old fort, as night fell on the plains, the trackers saw the flames of a fire, fueled by buffalo dung, a sign that their enemies could go no longer without rest. At dawn, the trackers intended to fall upon the sleeping men and dispatch them swiftly. Yet in the first light of day, the trackers found only the propped-up body of a dead Frenchman, left as though tending the fire, and one hobbled horse standing nearly dead on its feet.

"They outfoxed us, Barny," said the tall Indian in his native Abenaki to his companion. "Those two traveled all night and might reach the old fort before we do."

"Damnation" was the only reply. As they had with the other bodies, they quickly and carefully stripped the third man of any insignia, identifying papers, weapons, or jewelry by which he could be identified as a Frenchman. This body carried no gold. They freed the half-dead horse, mounted their own, and rode on in a hurry.

Barnabas Locke and Squando arrived at the old fort too late. Kansa people had long camped there for security and to trade at the post that flourished even as the old fort fell into disuse after the French handed over the territory to Spain. Two Kansa had found the struggling Frenchmen and delivered them to the proprietor of the post. Squando learned that both men were still alive, although the younger barely so.

Although both spoke French and had traded there for many years, they decided that Barnabas Locke, a white man known as the White Arapaho Man, should be their spokesman. Squando discreetly remained with the horses outside the stockade while Barnabas talked trade with the proprietor. The man's name was Deruisseau, the grandson of the French founder of the trading post. He was rank, fat, and loquacious, and he did love to talk with other white men, even those in native garb. He was interested in the deer hides and beaver pelts on Barnabas's packhorses, but first he wanted to bend his ear.

"I remember the older man. His name is Le-Blanc. He's likely to live. He first came here to the landing some three years ago as an agent for a great many Frenchmen. He said they were trappers. But it wasn't traps they wanted. They wanted horses, hundreds of them. My Kansa people alerted their trading partners to bring horses—sound, sturdy horses. This man LeBlanc inspected every one of them for fitness. He paid me in silver coin." Deruisseau paused for a long moment, sucking on hard sweets he popped into his almost toothless mouth. Then, abruptly, he changed tack.

"This man LeBlanc told me that two Indians pursued him. Are you and Squando, the Abenaki Prophet, those two Indians?"

Barnabas knew the nature of the man before him. "We are, but we were not in pursuit. These

3

men are not our business. Our aim was to come here to trade. I know I could get a better price in St. Louis, but it's a longer way. You interest me in this man LeBlanc. If he lives, would his safe arrival in St. Louis be worth it to you for the exchange of my trappings here? Or should I take my pelts to St. Louis? You say you know LeBlanc, but maybe other people who know him would be willing to pay a reward for his safe return. You said he paid in silver coin. Whose silver coin?"

As Barnabas allowed time for Deruisseau to mull over his proposition, he strolled to a heavy door and partly opened it. Within, a dead man lay with a blanket pulled over his face, and another man lay snoring on his back, his head resting on a leather pouch. Barnabas itched to open that pouch but quietly closed the door.

"You've got *one* man alive on your hands, Deruisseau," he said. "Tell me the rest of the story from three years ago."

The Frenchman resumed. "LeBlanc told me he had stopped at St. Louis long enough to order quantities of goods that would soon arrive on keel-boats at my landing. I had a private look, and none of those goods were traps. They were saws and hatchets, shovels and picks and wheelbarrows, kegs of gunpowder, Charleville muskets, winter clothes, and stacks of provisions. I stored them in the fort's old magazine; and when the men began to arrive,

I put those who would fit into the old barracks. More than three hundred men, not one of them a trapper, and four hundred horses all here eating and sleeping and shitting at my trading post. I was glad to see them gone, and, yes, LeBlanc paid in silver." Here followed a speculative pause. "We will do business here, and you will take LeBlanc to St. Louis. If a reward comes your way, you will pay me half for my troubles. Agreed?"

They shook hands. Then, Barnabas went outside and signaled to Squando, and they did business with the proprietor over the contents of the packs. They did not watch the burial of the dead man.

* * *

LeBlanc slept through the day and most of the night. In the hour before dawn, unsteady on his feet, he opened the door into the mercantile room, rousing Deruisseau, who had kept his own door open.

"Monsieur, I appreciate your hospitality, but I require a horse immediately. First, I need food and provisions to get me to St. Louis. Has my officer already been buried? I wish to deliver his personal effects to his family. I have silver coin." LeBlanc's voice had a deep, commanding timbre.

Deruisseau looked to the corner of the post, and LeBlanc followed his gaze. A lean, wiry figure in buckskins, a man of middling height with long dark hair clubbed at the back of his neck and a tomahawk on his right hip, emerged into the lamp light. LeBlanc uttered a sharp "Hah!"

Deruisseau hastily said, "Monsieur LeBlanc, may I introduce Monsieur Barnabas Locke, a business associate on his way to St. Louis, as are you. He has offered to escort you there. He is most trustworthy. To travel alone is too dangerous, especially for a man not at his best."

LeBlanc sneered. "He is an assassin."

"Not at all, not at all," Deruisseau assured him, flustered by the confidence of this Frenchman of whose fate he had washed his hands. Barnabas stepped forward and spoke in his passable French.

"You mistake me, Monsieur. I depart for St. Louis with or without you. My business in St. Louis is important. I cannot afford delays. But I assure you, you will not survive long traveling as a lone man through Osage country. Myself, I am on good terms with those giant warriors. I suggest you await the arrival of a keelboat headed back downriver." He turned politely to Deruisseau. "I saw no keelboats at the landing. The river runs high. When do you intend your next departure?"

"Oh, one can never be sure. Possibly three days from now? Four? All depends on the river. Then, one must allow for the arriving keelboat to be emptied and then reloaded." Deruisseau was the soul of cordial regret. He failed to mention that his own business had been concluded with Monsieur Locke.

"Gentlemen, I have broken fast and will step outside to attend to my horses. Monsieur Deruisseau, if Monsieur LeBlanc decides to accompany me, then will you kindly provide the necessary tack and provisions for his journey? If Monsieur can pay, so much the better. If not, to show good faith, I will go surety for the cost." With a slight bow, Barnabas left the post.

He smartly turned the corner and, out of sight, heaved up the light breakfast he had choked down. He inconveniently remembered that he had once assured a hard man that he was not an assassin and that, then, his denial had been true.

Squando appeared with three horses—Barnabas's mount already saddled, a packhorse convincingly loaded with travel provisions, and a third horse intended for LeBlanc. He laid a hand on Barnabas's shoulder and said in a low voice, "I will not be far away." He took a few steps and paused, turning his head to say, "It has to be done."

In short order, an old Kansa tacked up the third horse, under Deruisseau's watchful eye. LeBlanc, newly shaven, emerged from the post, and Barnabas noted that he carried his leather pouch cinched close under his arm. In sunlight, he saw that, even as gaunt as he was, LeBlanc was a handsome, well-set-up man in his prime, taller by a few inches than Barnabas.

Deruisseau watched the two men, uneasy companions, trot through the gates of the old fort, and turned with a shrug into his trading post.

* * *

"We follow the river's course for a few miles only and where the cliffs begin to fall, we leave the river and turn south and east towards St. Louis," Barnabas informed LeBlanc. He did not say that he had arranged with Squando to meet him where the cliffs fell. He steeled himself to finish his mission. He could sense LeBlanc's suspicion and resistance increasing.

"Perhaps you wish to hear something of my story?" LeBlanc inquired and began to speak in his deep voice.

"I was born in Normandy of a good family. I was educated for the diplomatic service, but my interests were always as a historian. At the siege of Toulon, I did a service for Citizen Paul Barras, born Vicomte de Barras and serving in a Royal regiment. He is now a powerful member of the Directory that rules all France. Alas, our new government, like your own, is without sufficient funds. Citizen Barras appointed me to join this mining expedition in the New World as its historian. In short, I was commissioned to provide a detailed report on the success or failure of this venture. I am duty bound to deliver it." With intent, he snugged the leather pouch tighter under his arm.

"I would like to hear what you have written in this report," Barnabas replied. "Your expedition harmed the Ute people, the Nuche. I, known as White Arapaho Man, live among the Utes. You trespassed on our lands to take gold without permission or payment. For many months, your miners hunted our game, shot our buffalo even in calving season—leaving to rot what they did not want. They tore the mountains open with gunpowder, diverting watercourses and offending the sacred spirits. Your miners frightened the women and children as they foraged. This spring, after the first thunderstorms, a party of your miners approached a band of Utes traveling peacefully to our Bear Dance. They offered our own gold to pay for the use of our women. My family—my wife and daughter and sister—were among these insulted women. Those nine men did not return. Your tribe has behaved like criminals. Do you report all that?" Barnabas nodded sharply at the leather pouch.

"So you *are* my assassin!" LeBlanc spat the words.

"Yes," Barnabas replied, "to keep the secrets of our mountains." He pulled his pistol from under his coat and aimed the fully cocked weapon at the Frenchman. "Get down," he barked.

"Hah, now we understand each other," said LeBlanc as he leisurely dismounted. With his back briefly to Barnabas, he slid a hidden knife down his sleeve.

Barnabas had also dismounted and pointed to the pouch. "The pouch, please." He pointed to his feet.

LeBlanc undid the strap and dangled the pouch at arm's length, directing Barnabas's attention to it. Then, LeBlanc threw the pouch with force at his assassin. As Barnabas instinctively caught the pouch by its strap, the weight threw him off-balance. In that instant, LeBlanc darted forward and thrust his knife into Barnabas's chest. Barnabas unsteadily raised the pistol in his hand, and LeBlanc grabbed it, twisting the muzzle away from his head. Yet the flash pan struck his forehead when the pistol discharged. As he fell, Barnabas had the satisfaction of seeing the powder from the flash pan scorch LeBlanc's face and hearing him scream.

Both wounded men heard the thunder of approaching hooves. A flurry of arrows thudded into the ground around LeBlanc's feet as he scrambled back onto his skittering horse. As Squando galloped nearer, a final arrow found its mark in LeBlanc's back. The Frenchman fell forward on his horse's neck as it bolted away.

Squando leaped down to attend to Barnabas. He was alive, but blood already soaked his chest.

As the sky twirled above him, he gasped, "Go after him, Squando. Quick, do what I could not." His face whitened under its stubble, his eyes fluttered, and he passed out of consciousness.

Squando looked after the fleeing man. LeBlanc still clung to his horse, already out of range of his arrows or Barnabas's rifle. Could LeBlanc survive, Squando questioned himself. "Yes," he said aloud, as a sudden vision of another confrontation appeared in his head. He knew then that Barnabas would live.

ONE

PLANS OF ACTION

August 1798 at a private house in Paris, France

"I assure you, Citizen Barras, the original map must have been buried with Lieutenant Benôit while I slept in exhaustion. And, as I have said, my report was lost when I was attacked by that murderous white Indian. Who else can recover the gold from its hiding places in those treacherous and distant mountains? This map in my hand was made while events were still fresh in mind. With my knowledge of the terrain, I am your man to lead the expedition you propose to underwrite. Indeed, in these past months, I have thought of nothing else." The tall man briefly fingered his scarred forehead.

Citizen Paul Barras, formerly the Vicomte de Barras and presently one of the five Directeurs of the newly constituted French government, considered the man before him. He noted with interest the burn mark on his forehead. He spun a convincing story, but could he be trusted with a fortune in gold at stake? If indeed the gold was actually hidden where only LeBlanc could find it?

"So, Citizen LeBlanc, what plan have you devised as you thought of nothing else?" His skepticism was concealed under a practiced suavity.

"First, a new approach from the south. As we are again on terms with the Spanish, I intend to disembark at New Orleans and go overland to Santa Fe in New Mexico territory. There supplies and fresh horses can be supplied by the Spanish. I made inquiries and have identified a merchant there. Fifty seasoned soldiers, I think, would be sufficient, allowing for attrition. The force would move fast and decisively." LeBlanc continued in this vein until Barras raised a languid hand to halt the rapid flow.

"This will be an expensive campaign, Citizen LeBlanc, and must be an entirely discreet one. If you are successful, you will not be hailed as a hero here in France, but you and your family will be wealthy. If you fail, no one will ever know your name, and no one must ever know that I financed a failed endeavor of this magnitude. La France has already poured a huge treasure of men and money into this disastrous affair. Yet, I believe the rewards would justify a second attempt." Paul Barras paused before he introduced a caveat.

"This is a military action and must be led by a military man with experience in mountainous terrain. I, too, have been making inquiries and have an officer at hand. As you may know, I rose to the rank of captain in the Regiment Royal Rousillon in those younger years when I served a king. Captain Gustave Rocher, a surly man to be sure, but from a distinguished military family and with the experience necessary, will serve my purposes. Rocher speaks Spanish, which should prove most useful."

LeBlanc was disappointed but not surprised. It might be for the best to have an officer in charge as he carried no rank himself. They discussed the orders to be undertaken by Rocher to handpick appropriate soldiers and to make the logistics as smooth and unremarked as possible. LeBlanc had no illusions about the patriotism of Citizen Paul Barras. The Directeur intended a make a fortune from this enterprise. LeBlanc intended revenge and the assurance of a comfortable life, even in these tumultuous times.

* * *

April 1799 at the Rancho Aguilar outside Santa Fe, New Mexico Territory

"Gold! What else could it be? Fifty bedraggled French soldiers, pretending not to be, arrive on your doorstep in Santa Fe, from God alone knows where, demanding fresh horses and provisions. What a charade! They believe those rumors of French gold miners in the mountains of Colorado."

Ramon Flores made the familiar calming gesture that irritated rather than calmed his sister. "Isabella, they want a guide too. I'm thinking of sending Ruiz."

"Not Ruiz!" Isabella rebutted sharply. "He is indispensable here on the rancho and too valuable a man to throw away on ruffians." She thought a moment and said more equably, "Do you really intend to do business with these Frenchmen?"

"I do, Isabella. The man LeBlanc, the man with the burn on his forehead, can pay in silver, always better than credit. But, more to my point, he asked me, in an offhand way, what did I know of one Barnabas Locke, who calls himself White Arapaho Man and lives among the Utes."

Isabella sucked in a deep breath and slowly expelled her shock with it. "What could he know of Barny? Why should he ask about him of all people? What more did he say?"

Ramon looked troubled. "He said Barnabas Locke has a wife and daughter and travels in the company of an Indian. This is why Ruiz must go, as someone we trust and who will remember Barny as a comrade in battle."

"I knew this man LeBlanc was trouble. We must get word to Barny immediately." She rang a bell on her desk and instructed the servant who silently appeared, "Find Señor Ruiz, he's likely at the stallion barn, and ask him to please come to the main house."

Doña Isabella of Rancho Aguilar was renowned for breeding horses from the best Spanish stock. In particular, she bred for bright chestnut horses with white markings—blaze, star, socks—and a spirited temperament. She and her daughters took great pleasure in naming the foals of each crop. Ruiz rode just such a horse, whom Isabella herself had named Pronto.

The three of them spent the afternoon discussing a plan of action. To ensure their privacy, Isabella dispatched her three young daughters, along with their governesses and armed servants, on an impromptu picnic.

The sister and brother disagreed vehemently on various points, but Ruiz, as he usually did, offered alternatives when the sister did not prevail outright. After thrashing out a course of action, Ruiz presented a summary for approval. He removed the wad of tobacco from his mouth.

"So, it is agreed that I will serve the French as guide with the mestizo Dominguez as scout. We delay their departure and then their progress by any means possible so that a message can be received by Señor Locke. There will be a regrettable delay in obtaining suitable horses to trade." He turned to

Doña Isabella and agreed with her, "Not one horse on this rancho will serve as a French mount, but I will put word out among the rancheros for what mounts and mules they can spare. The provisions that Señor Flores provides will be barely sufficient or not in stock. Señora, as you know English best, you will prepare the letter to Barnabas Locke to be delivered through the Arapaho, Two Rivers." He nodded to Ramon. "A good idea, sir. Two Rivers is not only your secret trading partner, but he is a fellow Red Circle warrior with Señor Locke."

Ramon broached the subject they were all dancing around, "And what about the gold, should there be any?"

Ruiz replied eagerly, "It could go to support the cause of Mexican independence, which we all strongly encourage, privately of course."

But Ramon refuted this reasoning. "Gold only serves to corrupt. For such a glistening, pretty thing, it brings nothing but corruption and shame. The Spanish government must ascribe no motive in this endeavor other than honest commerce between Casa de Flores in Santa Fe and the Spanish-speaking Captain Rocher. The name LeBlanc need not figure in any receipts."

Isabella cautioned, "It is well to remember that our personal stake in this matter is the safety of our old friend and comrade Barnabas Locke and his family. If the rumors prove true and a French expedition of gold miners, mysteriously vanished to a man, did succeed in finding gold, that gold belongs only to the Utes." She and her brother exchanged a look meaningful only to themselves. In his youth, Ramon had once suffered a bout of gold fever that nearly cost him his honor.

That evening, Isabella pulled from a chest a small leather pouch she had worked during a long-ago summer on the plains. With clever fingers, she unstitched the beads and quills and reassembled them to indicate a man on horseback riding towards a white man with a red circle on his shoulder and an arrow pointing to mountains. To its recipient, Two Rivers, that message would be clear. He must quickly take the pouch unopened to his brother warrior living among the Mountain Utes. On her best paper and with her best ink, she wrote the following carefully chosen words:

23 April 1799. To Barnabas Locke, the White Arapaho Man, from Ramon Flores and Isabella Aguilar. A French expedition of 50 armed men departs Santa Fe soon to recover gold buried in the mountains of the Utes. Captain Rocher leads the corps, but its real leader is LeBlanc, a man with an ugly scar across his forehead. Barny, this man knows your name and that you have a Ute family. The guide is our Corporal Ruiz. He will delay them by any means. Make sure he comes to no harm.

Isabella tucked the folded paper into the pouch and then, on a whim as a gift or perhaps as a private message, she took an object from her bureau top that she had used since girlhood and dropped it with a smile into the pouch.

After Isabella presented the pouch to Ramon, he read and sealed the letter and replaced it in the pouch. He smiled briefly as his fingers touched the object lying at the bottom. It gave him a thought. He went to his bed chamber and opened a chest. Atop the buckskins he had worn that long-ago summer while a guest of the Arapaho lay the eagle feather Two Rivers had given him as they had once parted company. Pulling the strings of the pouch tight and knotting them, he inserted into the knot the shaft of the feather. With a dab of hot wax, he sealed the string and feather together.

* * *

21st April 1799 at Philadelphia, Pennsylvania

In his second-floor rooms in Mrs. Smith's boardinghouse on Spruce Street, U.S. Senator Edward "Ned" Locke of Vermont met that afternoon with Treasury Secretary Oliver Wolcott and his younger brother Captain Enoch Locke, a veteran of the campaign against the Northwest Indians. The younger Locke had been kicking his heels waiting for a new posting back in the territories.

"Gentlemen, I am about to read you a message lately received from an agent operating in New Orleans. Its purport leads to some interesting possibilities." The senator donned his spectacles and read aloud:

"1st April, 1799. Have noted the disembarkment of 52 Frenchmen, not in uniform but soldiers under the command of Captain Gustave Rocher, from the French merchant ship, "*Bonchance*," sailing from the Atlantic port La Rochelle on 25 February 1799. To wit: I sought out one of these men in a port side tavern and plied him with rum. In his cups, he confided that he would be wealthy when he returned to France. He spoke incoherently of a recovery mission in mountains, that he had been picked because he was born in the Pyrenees, and that his commander was a miserable *enfant de chienne*. I discounted any value in his ramblings until I learned that his throat had been cut later that night. I sought out another of these Frenchmen in a brothel. I spare you the particulars, but the upshot was that he had been picked for a mission because he spoke Spanish and would be useful in Santa Fe and that he had served in mountainous campaigns. He, too, disparaged his commander. But he did express confidence in a civilian named LeBlanc with an ugly burn scar across his forehead. This French contingent, of whatever nature, departed overland in the general direction of Santa

Fe early this morning, minus two of their original number. I will cast my net wider and report any further intelligence. We are all aware that relations between our governments are under severe strain."

Senator Locke dropped the paper onto his desk and took off his spectacles. "That is the gist of the matter at hand. It might well be relegated to the files but for the particular name LeBlanc. That name surfaced nearly four years ago when reports reached my desk that a very large contingent of Frenchmen, mainly miners, had reached the mountains of the Colorado and yet were never seen again. The sole exception was a man named LeBlanc, bearing an angry burn on his face, who turned up late last summer in St. Louis. He booked passage there to New Orleans and was noted in a dispatch received from my old colleague Joshua Jones. My instincts tell me there is something here, gentlemen, and that something concerns gold. Your thoughts, Mr. Secretary?"

Treasury Secretary Wolcott cleared his throat, took a sip of water, and addressed the question. "We are sorely strapped, as you well know. You, Captain Locke, are doubtless on half-pay. Our government moves next year to our new Capitol, and the smallest expenditure will be scrutinized. This seems on its face a hare-brained venture based on very little fact and a great deal of imaginative speculation. In other times, I would quash it in its infancy. However, if there is gold to be found in our own backyard, it would grieve me to see it carried off by the French, however much I esteem them for their aid in our late war of independence. I can put my hands on a small sum to be spent *very conservatively* in pursuit of more intelligence."

Captain Locke uncrossed his long legs and leaned forward. "What purpose am I to serve in this affair, Brother? I am in dire need of action and place myself at your disposal."

"Enoch, you are already at my disposal. Your commanding officer and I spoke yesterday. You are seconded to my office for an indefinite period of time. In short, I am issuing you orders, and you will depart for St. Louis two days hence. It's little time, I know, but time is of the essence. Your mission is twofold. First, to ascertain the value of this report," and here he tapped the paper on his desk. "If gold is the quest of these fifty-some Frenchmen, then you are authorized to, shall we say, *appropriate* it before it leaves our shores. You will take a cadre of three men, men of your own choosing, across the Mississippi to St. Louis. There, you will consult with a very useful man, the merchant Mr. Joshua Jones. You might remember that name from tales of my short military career that I regaled you with when you were a boy."

Secretary Wolcott coughed. "I think I must take my leave as you two gentlemen discuss the particulars of this venture. Perhaps I am best left in ignorance. I do suggest, my dear Senator, that you relinquish that intimidating weapon you carry on your hip. I think it will serve a better purpose carried by your brother into country a little more hostile, but only a little so, than the Senate floor." He turned to Enoch. "Tomorrow, I will place in your hands a sum in silver rather than in scrip, undocumented, although I expect you to account for any expense beyond this amount." The secretary rose, took up his beaver tall hat, and let himself out.

"And what is the second part of my mission?" Enoch asked.

"The Secretary is right, Enoch. I've carried this tomahawk since I was fourteen years old, but never used it against another man. The one time I was taken unawares, it wasn't on my hip. You've admired it since boyhood. As you know, it has a twin, carried by your cousin Barnabas. Enoch, find him. That is your second mission. Jones has sent me the occasional message over the years, and we know that Barny still lives and lives among the Arapaho or perhaps the Utes, as he has married a Ute woman and has a daughter by her. So little to know of someone I knew so well. Relay to him our births and deaths and give to him this damnable sack I have carried for nearly twenty years as an obligation to Zeke's Abenaki wife Molly. She promised Barnabas a new pair of moccasins each year in token payment for his family homestead. Each year this sack grew heavier."

"I remember the story, Ned. I've watched Molly at work upon them. It will be my honor to deliver them at last now that poor Molly is dead."

TWO

A WOMAN'S GIFT

May 1799 at a Ute village in the mountains of central Colorado.

Juniper leaned her back against a cottonwood, providing shade along the creek running through the horse pasture. A massive dog, his shiny coat as black as a raven's wing, sat in watch beside her. Boys, Squando's middle son among them, were busy among the horses, aware of her presence. As her hands wove horsehair into lengths of rope for bridles, Juniper mused over a particular dappled gray horse, more than fifteen hands high. His Spanish blood was evident in his deeply dished face, the short back, and powerful haunches. His long mane and full tail were black. His coat would nicely show off painted symbols.

Juniper had hopes for this horse. He was showy, but solid and responsive. The gray was also aware of her presence and slowly drifted closer to her.

The black dog was eager to teach this horse that it was he who determined who would approach his mistress. The dog leaned his heavy weight against her leg. Juniper smiled and made the signal he was waiting for. "Bring him in, Cuervo," and she waved toward the gray horse. Cuervo bounded forward. The horse lowered his handsome head and shook it defiantly at the dog, but moved obligingly towards the cottonwood with the black dog at his heels.

This gray horse, she thought, might be a worthy successor to the elderly bay horse rooted in her husband's heart. She feared that heart would break when Little Bay died. The White Arapaho Man had mourned an unseemly long time for the Spanish dog Amigo, grandsire of Cuervo. A cairn of flat stones marked the dog's burial site, as one would in time mark the gravesite of the bay horse. The stones were already gathered.

The gray had been among the horses allotted by the elders to their Ute band after the cleansing of the French miners from the mountains. She had watched the gray come into his full strength over the past year and had set her heart on him as the one who would win her husband's affections. Although her husband's body had healed from the knife wound that had nearly killed him, she feared that her husband's long brooding would worsen with the inevitable death of Little Bay. No healing sweat or curing ceremony would abolish that depression. She needed this horse to be ready. Much of her gentling and training time with the horses had been lost while she had been devoted to her husband's recovery. But she had made time to train this horse in Ute ways. Now, the White Arapaho Man seemed to quietly push her away. He refused to confide in her the cause of his inner misery. She suspected, in fact she knew, that Squando could tell her and also that he would never reveal the secrets of the friend of his youth.

Her mind dismissed these troubling thoughts as she spoke to the gray through her hands. With a whisk of knotted grasses, she rubbed his body clean, reaching even the ticklish places under his belly. She tapped each knee as a signal for him to raise that hoof, praising him lavishly when he rested it briefly in her cupped hand. She combed through his thick mane with her fingers and pulled bits of brush from his tail. His head dropped and his eyes closed as he surrendered to her hands.

Leaning at last against the gray's shoulder, soothed in spirit, her repose was broken by a sudden burst of activity in the horse pasture. The boys had flung themselves bareback upon war ponies and were galloping down the horse pasture and through the village, whooping exuberantly. Cuervo unleashed a volley of deep-throated barks, joining the chorus of the village dogs below. A visitor had arrived and awaited permission to enter. Juniper flung the coil of horsehair rope over her shoulder, and with Cuervo running ahead, hurried down the horse pasture, making the hopeful hand sign for good news.

She recognized the figure of the mounted man and his horse, too, just as she knew every horse once it had come to her attention. The pinto was vividly painted with blue symbols, but neither horse nor man wore war paint. The man was the Arapaho chief, Two Rivers, her husband's friend and fellow member in the warrior society of their age group.

"Here is Two Rivers come a long way. He has a message for my uncle," a little boy proudly called to her. This chubby, cheerful child, youngest son of Squando and Singing Grass, was dear to her.

Juniper shooed away the crowd of mounted youths. The dogs, satisfied that the intruder was welcome, went back to their pursuits. The women and children remained close by to hear what news had brought this distinguished Arapaho to their village.

"White Arapaho Man is not here, Two Rivers," she said to the mounted man. "Come rest yourself and your horse. I expect them back by nightfall, and you are welcome to stay with us." She hailed a passing boy and ordered him to take the spent pinto, remove his tack, rub him down, and put him in the brush shelter with a corral reserved for Little Bay. "Take enough fresh-cut grass for them both," she called after him. "And close the gate."

Juniper suppressed her curiosity and politely led Two Rivers to her tipi. Her daughter, Sky Feather, left a group of young women who had been cutting out patterns from dressed deer hide. Sky Feather, a confident girl, greeted her father's friend as an uncle and in good Arapaho. Squando's soft-spoken wife, Singing Grass, beckoned them to her cook pot full of savory stew, natural to a woman feeding a husband and three sons.

When satisfied, Juniper and Two Rivers stepped aside, and Juniper sat down on a smoothly worn log. Two Rivers quietly inquired as to the health of his old friends. The White Arapaho Man and the Abenaki Prophet Squando had spent a summer long ago with the Arapahos, earning the privilege and the prestige of initiation into the Red Circle cohort as Arapaho warriors. The three men bore the tattoos of that society on their shoulders. Their bonds went deep. They hunted buffalo together. Squando had brought his gravely wounded friend to his village on the grasslands for healing by the famed Blue Smoke, who had long ago saved the life of the young Spaniard, Ramon Flores.

"Before dawn today, White Arapaho Man, Squando, and Squando's eldest son went with the other men to check their beaver traps. If all has gone well, they will be back by nightfall. This is the first time he has gone in company since he returned from your village. He goes off alone for long hours, and he speaks little. More to Sky Feather than to me. Two Rivers, my husband is still sick in his spirit. Perhaps you bring a message that will do him good."

Two Rivers thought carefully. "This pouch was delivered to me from Santa Fe. What it holds must be important. The message comes from our old friend Ramon Flores. Perhaps the White Arapaho Man has spoken of him?" Juniper shook her head.

She held out her hand for the pouch, and hesitantly, Two Rivers put it into her hand. She closely examined the soft leather, the care with which the pouch had been fashioned, and traced the reworked pattern of the beads and quills with curious fingers. She recognized the handiwork of a skilled woman. With reverence, she stroked the vanes of the sacred eagle feather. Two Rivers responded to her look of inquiry.

"I took that feather from my head to give to Ramon Flores when we parted. He was very young then, and I hoped it would remind him to keep his word in all things. The White Arapaho Man kept his promise to guide him and his sister to safety in Santa Fe."

Juniper nodded with new understanding. "My husband is an honorable man. You saw the meaning worked into this pouch and brought it to your brother. What it contains is bad news," she said decisively and handed the pouch, unopened, back to Two Rivers.

"The White Arapaho Man is my brother and his wife and family will always be welcome among us Arapaho." It was an invitation that Juniper took to her heart.

While it was still light, the trapping party returned. The White Arapaho Man gladly greeted Two Rivers, shaking his old friend by the shoulders. "I recognized your horse eating grass with Little Bay. Two Rivers, you have come on an errand, but first come see these beaver pelts. Choose one to take home to Tiva for your trouble. She will roast its tail as a feast for your return." Juniper, relieved to see her husband in good spirits, left the two old friends and beckoned Sky Feather to join her in conversation with Singing Grass. Cuervo chose to accompany his master.

She discreetly watched as Squando joined the two men, and they walked together in close companionship to the horse pasture. She saw the pouch change hands and the eagle feather be returned to Two Rivers. Then they disappeared under the cottonwoods. Night had just fallen when they returned. She was surprised that it was Squando who was giving sleeping space to Two Rivers, not her husband. She heard him order Cuervo to stay with Little Bay. He entered their tipi with a short greeting to her and asked Sky Feather to visit one of her friends. The girl cast an inquiring look at her mother, who merely nodded her head. The White

Arapaho Man sat down by the fire, moodily stirring the embers back into flame.

"What is the news, Husband? Tell me what it means for us. Don't shut me out of your thoughts," Juniper urged.

"Yes," he confirmed, "the message does concern us. It concerns all of us. Friends have sent a warning from Santa Fe to me and to our people. I will read it to you." He read slowly, translating the English words. When it was read, he folded the paper and slipped it back into the pouch, where his fingers touched an object at the bottom.

He pulled out a tortoiseshell comb and burst into laughter, the first time she had heard him laugh since the cleansing in the mountains. He held the comb aloft and presented it to her with a flourish.

"I think this is a gift for you."

THREE

THE NUCHE GATHER

"I will have to speak the truth. It was my mission to kill him. I failed. Still, I thought it likely he was dead." Barnabas spoke in a mix of resignation, shame, and frustration. He could speak in this way only with Squando, whom he trusted in all things.

"We both hoped he was dead, Barny," Squando replied. "When you hesitated to shoot him, you failed. When I chose to save your life rather than take his, I failed. When I took you to the Osage to staunch your bleeding, they said they would find and kill him. They failed. There were many failures. One man triumphed. The failures are behind us." It was good advice, but, in truth, Squando also acutely felt the sting of failure.

The two were determined to acquit themselves as honorable men, a white man and an Abenaki, both natives of the woodlands to the far east. They approached the council fire blazing in the midst of a ceremonial space, surrounded by the tipis of those gathered on behalf of the eleven bands of the Nuche. They were respected elders, war chiefs, notable medicine men, famed drummers, and to Barnabas's keen displeasure, the aggressive and arrogant warrior High Winds. All these years later, this Ute still limped, but only in Barnabas's presence, to remind him that High Winds remained his sworn enemy. Barnabas and Squando had a plan to present, but consensus would be required to put it into action. Here would be one voice raised against any plan Barnabas endorsed. They judged it wiser that the highly respected Squando speak for them both.

When each man had taken his first long puff of sacred tobacco from the pipes passed hand to hand, Walking Man rose and began to speak. He had eminence among them. He was a known warrior, orator, and storyteller, and had served for many years as the Cat Man at the annual Bear Dance. After naming each of the influential Utes in turn, he acknowledged the presence of the Arapaho Two Rivers and invited him to speak.

Two Rivers, a seasoned diplomat in his dealings with the neighboring Utes, spoke respectfully. "I am honored by the invitation to speak on this matter. My friendship with the White Arapaho Man and the Abenaki Prophet, Squando, is long. Many years ago, while still young men, they were brought to our village by the revered warrior

Young Raven. As we are taught, the bloodlines of all our many peoples run together like tributaries to a great river." A murmur of approval arose. He continued. "I fought Kiowas with those young men. I hunted buffalo with them. I taught them the ways of our Red Circle society of warriors. I listened to their stories of the war against a great king in their homeland. I negotiated with them on behalf of an unwise young Spaniard under their protection who had trespassed on Ute lands. In all things, they were brave and active and honorable. The foolish Spaniard, whom I took south out of Arapaho territory, is the same grown man who has sent the warning, through me, to the White Arapaho Man. I pledge that my warriors will protect the eastern flank of Ute territory from any trespass by foreigners of any nation. If we can do more, we will come to your aid. I leave your councils as a friend and ally." Two Rivers judged that his words had been well received and withdrew.

Walking Man allowed time for the rustling to subside, coughed, and then resumed, his sonorous voice accompanied by the eloquent gestures of his hand talk.

"Since the cleansing from our sacred Mother Earth of those many Frenchmen, as many as a small herd of buffalo, we have each sought to restore balance with the spirits of all nature, among our villages, and within ourselves. Those terrible days left both our numbers and our souls diminished. Widows and fatherless children were made, here in our own lands and in places we will never see. We bore their injuries and insults for a long time, but when the sacred nature of our Bear Dance had been violated by these men, then honor demanded they pay with their lives. I was sad that many familiar faces were not among us for this year's Bear Dance." Here, he was silent for a long moment. He resumed.

"We continue to seek healing in mind and spirit. Each of us has called upon our women to sing good songs and to prepare curative medicines. Our medicine men conduct ceremonies to purge bad feelings. In our sweat lodges, to the rhythm of our drummers, we seek purification around the sacred fire. Some of us make pilgrimage to the sacred mountain Tava and to the healing waters of the springs at Manitou. We have prayed and sought visions to guide us. We have told this terrible story in the buffalo hides of our winter count. We do not forget. If this new force of Frenchmen who come for gold are not stopped, we must then fight again, leaving more dead to profane our lands. Squando, the Abenaki Prophet, what do your visions tell you?"

Squando rose to speak. He accompanied his words with hand talk so that all would understand. His voice was quiet but reached every listening ear. "First, I admit that my brother, the White Arapaho Man, and I failed to end the life of the Frenchman LeBlanc, attempting to escape justice for his crimes. The White Arapaho Man failed with the pistol he fired into his face. I failed with the arrow I planted in his back. To save the life of my brother, I took him to the Osage and set them to find LeBlanc's body. In this, the Osage failed. We all believed he had died and his body rotted on the grasslands. We had taken from him the words he had put down on paper and the map he carried that led to the hidden gold. These we burned. Even had he lived, we believed he had no power to return. We deceived ourselves with what we wanted to be so. This admission I freely make, on behalf of the White Arapaho Man and myself." He paused as his admission of guilt swept through the assembly.

"To make amends, we have devised a plan that will end this threat of gold seekers." Squando raised his hand to signal the importance of what he had to say. He cogently laid out the plan that he and Barnabas had first conceived in the immediate aftermath of the cleansing. Up to a certain point, his listeners nodded in appreciation of its daring and cleverness. But when Squando said in conclusion, "The visions that appear clearly in my mind, whether my eyes are closed or open, show me a confrontation that ends with the words, "Go home." I see the backs of men in retreat. I see a dark and smothering cloud descend upon them.

I see their destruction not by our hands, but by the powers of all the sacred spirits turned in wrath against them. I see the natural order return to our lives, at least for a time." A moment of stunned silence was followed by an uproar of dissent, led vociferously by High Winds, who leaped out of turn to his feet.

"They must die to a man! Who among us believes otherwise?" And here he pointed an accusatory finger straight at Barnabas. "He does! Yes, your plan is good. But it must not end as you want. This man, by his own admission, permitted an enemy to elude our trap, and why, because he could not stomach killing one of his own. I have no problem killing white men. Now, because of this man's failure, we Nuche must defend ourselves against more Frenchmen. The White Arapaho Man names himself as an Arapaho. He bears the tattoo of an Arapaho. His friend who speaks for him is an Arapaho. His friend Squando is an Abenaki. Marriage into a Ute family," and here High Winds tread a little softer, "does not make him a Ute. I say the Arapahos may have him. But we Nuche ban him. He is a white man and has no place at our councils." Some of his listeners looked slyly at Walking Man, who was a blood relative of the White Arapaho Man's wife, but that impassive face registered nothing.

High Winds had more to say. "And Squando is filled with crazy notions. My name is High Winds, but I do not deceive myself that I have the power to blow away other men at will. Stick to the plan and kill our enemies."

Other Utes rose to speak, most in favor of killing the Frenchmen. Some counseled against a massacre, foreseeing another collapse of balance with Mother Earth. They liked Squando's vision of the natural spirits meting out their own vengeance. A few, including Buffalo Bones, another loyal friend, defended the White Arapaho Man as a man worthy of his standing among both the Arapaho and the Nuche. At length, Walking Man dismissed the council, urging the dignitaries to consider what they had heard, to discuss the matter with other minds, and to attend tomorrow prepared to come to a consensus.

After the White Arapaho Man and Squando emerged from the crowd, speaking quietly together, Squando's eldest son, Growler's Cub, fell into step with them. He had heard the plan proposed from outside the circle. He spoke earnestly to his father, but looked to his uncle for support in his cause. "Make me one of the scouts sent south to watch for the Frenchmen. In the great cleansing, I stripped the bodies of the dead. I gathered muskets, shot, and powder horns. Then, Father, you set me to rounding up horses and guarding them in Big Box Canyon. This time, I want to do a warrior's duty, not a youth's."

FOUR

DOWN THE GOOD RIVER

Captain Enoch Locke looked into a distracting pair of bright blue eyes. He stood at the broad counter at Bellevue's Dry Goods Store on the dockside where he had bought provisions and now sought a speedy departure from the newly named city of Pittsburgh.

"Yes," he said, forcing his mind back to business, "I want to hire a keelboat to take me downriver as quick as this minute to Fort Massac. No landings for pick-ups or drop-offs."

The young woman with the yellow hair and the bright blue eyes looked thoughtful, glancing down at the receipt she had written for his goods. "You *are* in a hurry, Mr. Locke. Here at Bellevue's, we book passengers and carry freight, delivered and picked up all along the Ohio. Not much call for a keelboat for only one passenger and not much in the way of freight." She smiled despite herself at the impatient but handsome man with a military bearing before her. She tapped a finger on the counter.

"Mike Fink's back on the docks, a little the worse for wear. But then when isn't he? He runs the best crew on the Ohio, and he makes his own bookings. He'd be the one willing to take your hire." She made up her mind and opened the countertop. "I'll take you down to the *Gullywhumper* and tell you, whilst we walk, about Mike Fink, our king of the keelboaters. He's a big man with a loud voice and a rowdy nature, and he does love a fight." She called a boy to tend the counter and another to trundle her customer's purchases behind them. Piled on top was Enoch's tack; the tired horse had been sold to a livery.

Enoch liked the look of her; he liked her smile, her trim sturdy figure. He liked her cheerful manner. "But I'm more interested in you, Miss Bellevue. Mr. Fink can wait. Tell me about yourself. You know my name. By rights, I should know yours."

She laughed and pointed to the sign above the store. "My name is Bellevue, Marguerite Bellevue, but friends call me Daisy. That's what Marguerite means in French. It might not be my born name. I was a child taken by Wyandots and never claimed by my real folks. But I was lucky. The Bellevues at the trading post upriver at Kittanning took me in and treated me as kin. They left me this store when they died. But I'd like to be shut of the smoke and spit and scallywags. Some day, I'm going to sell up and go down the Ohio myself, like all these starry-eyed, grass-green settlers. Maybe take the ferry across the Mississip to St. Louis. I know a merchant there, name of Jones, who has fingers in every pie. He'd help me set up a shop selling, oh, maybe ladies' wear. Nice things like gloves and muffs, bonnets, hatpins, and pretty fabrics."

Daisy chatted on as they strode down the docks, introducing herself to this interesting man before he was gone downriver and likely out of her life. "Now, that's enough about me. I never spoke so much about myself in all my life. You're a good listener, Mr. Locke. That boat there, the one with the patched sail, that's the *Gullywhumper*, and I've yet to tell you about our snapping turtle, Mike Fink. I wish you good luck." She held out her hand for him to shake in goodbye.

Enoch took the friendly hand and held it longer than was strictly polite. "The name Bellevue seemed familiar to me, and so I turned right in. The why of it will come to me, I expect. A great pleasure to meet you, Miss Bellevue. When my business is done, I will ask about you in St. Louis, and if you are not there, then here at Bellevue's Dry Goods Store." His brown eyes looking straight into her bright blue ones, he lifted the ink-stained fingers briefly to his lips. After an instant of surprise, she said demurely, "You *are* in a hurry, Mr. Locke," followed by a peal of merry laughter.

Neither noticed the big, rough man standing on the deck of the *Gullywhumper*, scowling and clenching his hands.

As Daisy Bellevue had warned, Mike Fink did have a loud voice. It clanged like a blacksmith's hammer in Enoch's ears.

"Down to Fort Massac by yerself, ye say? Just this piddling pile of goods, ye say? Make it worth my time, ye say, but it ain't jist my time. We go with a crew of six—best polers on the river, Ohio or Mississip, and not one of 'em good as me. Thems are here about, likely in a bawdyhouse or sleeping off last night's hurrah. Mebbe they'll show and mebbe not." He waved a dismissive hand to encompass all the dockside. But his eyes glistened when Enoch withdrew a small leather pouch from an inner pocket and shook out a satisfactory number of silver coins into his palm.

Enoch passed the coins over into Fink's huge, calloused hand. Then he said, "The rest of these if you get me to Fort Massac in under thirty days." Enoch restored the pouch to his pocket, clinking the coins enticingly.

Within the hour, the *Gullywhumper* embarked with a full crew and a passenger of one. Enoch stretched out on the cabin roof, weary to the bone. He had set himself and the horses he had ridden a blistering pace to cover in eight days the nearly four hundred miles between Philadelphia and Pittsburgh. He yearned for sleep. Yet in this company, he doubted he would close both eyes the length of the Ohio. When he was kicked awake, he nearly rolled off the cabin roof. The *Gullywhumper*, riding fast with her light load and rounding a bend, raced on the high current straight for the embrace of a floating "catcher," a massive sycamore, one of the old giants, that had entangled debris and was now about to capture the keelboat. Mike Fink filled his lungs and bellowed orders.

"All hands to starboard. Set 'n push! Set 'n push! Set 'n push! Rudder man, hard to port! Hard, do ye hear me! Are ye deaf, man? Locke, are ye on a pleasure cruise? Help that rudder man!" Together, Enoch and the rudder man at the stern heaved mightily against the rudder's arm in a frantic effort to avoid entanglement. But the current ran too fast, and branches reached out to strike the bow, knocking the first of the pole setters into the river. Enoch, quick to act, reached down over the gunnels and grasped the man by his hair as he bobbed past. He pulled the hapless man closer to the boat and heaved him higher out of the murky water. Fink, cursing ungodly words, jumped down from the cabin and seized a flailing arm. They pulled the dazed man aboard, like landing a Mississippi catfish. It was done in the last possible moment.

Everyone ducked as branches scraped across the bow and down the starboard side, the pole setters leaping for safety. But the current that had gotten them into this fix now saved them. They outran the debris catcher and left it behind another bend.

"Yer a jinx!" Mike Fink yelled into Enoch's face, his spittle flying. "Ye nearly cost me the *Gullywhumper*!"

"But I saved your man," Enoch snapped back.

"Ye left your post without orders. Ye put the *Gullywhumper* in danger and coulda lost us all." In a fury that he owed the life of one of his crew to this landlubber, Fink turned on Enoch, seizing his chance to put this highfalutin Easterner in his place.

"If ye want to get to Fort Massac in such a goldurned hurry, ye can pick up that pole yerself and do an honest man's work."

So, this was the king of the keelboaters, Enoch thought sourly, just as Daisy, and he did think of her as Daisy, had tried to warn him. A braggart and a bully. From what he, as a landsman, could tell, the keelboat was badly scraped, but didn't seem to be taking on water. The pole setter had been knocked hard on his even harder head, but he had not drowned.

Enoch dearly wanted to throw a punch into that spitting face, but his quick temper had been regulated by military discipline. He steadied himself by recalling his mission and went forward to the bow and picked up the pole without another word.

By day's end, his shoulders burning and his palms cracking, Enoch had a new appreciation for the labors of a pole setter. Already past first dark, Fink put the *Gullywhumper* into a landing lit by a lantern as a guide for keelboats. The landing was at a narrow shallows in the broad, meandering river.

After a dinner of fried fish and beans with a heap of stale cornbread, Enoch was more than ready to turn in. As a paying passenger, Enoch felt entitled to sleep in the cabin. Fink thought otherwise.

"The cabin's for passengers. Ain't ye a pole setter now?" He flung the taunt like a little knife.

Already wearied of the man, Enoch replied, "In this bunch, maybe it's smarter to sleep atop my goods."

And thus it would go—insult for insult, taunt for taunt—down the broad bosom of the Ohio to liberty at Fort Massac.

In the night, when he rose to relieve himself over the gunnels, he saw lantern lights bobbing across the water. He heard the shush a woman makes to a fretful child. He leaned over, listening intently. He heard small splashes and a muffled cough. The rudder man was smoking a pipe on the cabin roof. It was his watch. He noted Enoch's sudden interest and called down softly, "Black folks cross here in the night. White folks who don't hold with that institution help 'em on their way north. They call the Ohio the River Jordan." Enoch nodded to the rudder man and turned away with a sudden image of Zeke and Molly's son in his mind.

On his second day of duty as a pole setter, Enoch paid more attention to the mechanics of the work. Along the gunnels ran a cleated footway, maybe eighteen inches wide, that the crew walked as they plied their poles. Each pole setter carried a pole some twenty feet long and positioned himself on the footway on the shore side, about five feet apart to give each other sufficient room. Enoch learned to set the pole firmly on the river bottom and rest the upper part against his shoulder. With the others, he walked the sixty feet to the aft end of the footway with a strong and steady step, giving the boat a great push forward. At the stern, each man walked back to the bow and set his pole anew.

"Why not set the sail? Wouldn't that move us along quicker?" Enoch asked the rudder man, whose name was Tugger. For whatever reason, he had appointed himself Enoch's tutor on all things about the river.

"The river runs high this time of year what with snowmelt pouring down the creeks. Mike Fink can recite the name of every one of 'em in proper order. He often does. Tisn't just water coming down 'em; it all sorts of lumber and trash." Finally, Tugger got around to answering the question. "The current is in our favor but the wind ain't. The sail would set the *Gullywhumper* at odds with the river. Would block the line of sight anyways. Better to use the sail comin' upriver, if the wind's blowing right a'course." Tugger relit his pipe, a signal that he was done talking.

Another time, Tugger, without being asked, offered an opinion of his captain. "Mike Fink reads the river like the back of his hand—the channels, shallows, bends, eddies and whirlpools, deadheads and catchers, sandbars, all of it. This river keeps no secrets from Mike Fink." Tugger chuckled. "I expect that's why he's king of the keelboaters."

Enoch learned respect for the prowess of Mike Fink, though not for his character. Always, the man was vigilant for catchers and deadheads, those logs lodged in the mud of the river bed, ready to impale an unwary craft. He was also alert for dangers of another kind. Pirates plied their unsavory trade along the Ohio. His reputation kept them at bay; crossing Mike Fink was not worth the risk. But Fink kept a night watch on duty as good policy.

As the *Gullywhumper* swiftly passed the bulky, awkward flatboats, loaded with settlers, livestock, and goods, her crew was greeted with cheerful waves and banter. Tugger told him, "Them flatboats get took apart when they get to where they be going. Ain't worth hauling 'em back upriver. The planks get made into cabins or sold outright."

Another time, Tugger said in a musing voice, "The Senecas named this river the "O-hi-yo." It means somethin' like "Good River," which I guess is about right."

On his monotonous round of pole-setting, Enoch noted the changing landscape as it seemed to drift past. Much of the hillsides down to the river banks had been stripped of lush old forest; the trees had gone to build the settlements, the farms, and the landings, dotting the riverbank on both sides. At the landings, the firstcomers paused to watch the boats go by, tossing out free advice to the settlers headed farther downriver or beyond to the Mississippi. It was free entertainment, and many lively exchanges crossed the water in the fleeting moments of passage. If he lived long enough, Enoch intended to tell a particular story about Mike Fink.

A farmer, tipsy with a jug cradled in his arms, wobbled down to his landing. "Is that you, Mike Fink? I knowed it by yer bellowing, bragging, bullying voice clear upriver two miles away."

"It's me, alright, ye polecat. Ye're drunk on skunk piss."

"I drink to your death, Mike Fink," and the farmer defiantly hoisted the jug high above his thirsty mouth.

Like a lightning strike, the jug exploded above his head, showering him with corn whiskey, shards, and froth.

As the *Gullywhumper* sped by, the man shouted obscenities and shook his fist impotently.

Swaggering, Mike Fink handed his rifle to Tugger and bellowed back, "I coulda shot yer ear off if I was of a mind."

He turned to Enoch and hooted the most fantastical boasting Enoch had ever heard, "I can out-run, out-jump, out-shoot, out-brag, out-drink, an' out-fight, rough-an'-tumble, no holts barred, ary man on both sides the river from Pittsburgh to New Orleans an' back again to St. Louiee. I love the women an' I'm chockful o' fight! I'm half wild horse and half cockeyed-alligator and the rest o' me is crooked snags an' red-hot snappin' turtle. I'm Mike Fink, king of the keelboaters. Don't ye forgit it, Enoch Locke. Cock-a-doodle-doo!"

Finally, as they neared Louisville, a flourishing settlement on the Kentucky side of the river, the mended pole setter reclaimed his pole. Enoch was happy to relinquish it and relieved that he would not be on duty as the *Gullywhumper* descended the infamous Falls of the Ohio. The Falls were the only natural obstacle to navigation on the long, meandering course of this beautiful river. Once the Falls were successfully navigated, he need endure the obstreperous Mike Fink for only the final run to his departure point, Fort Massac, newly rebuilt on the southern boundary of the Illinois Territory.

Tugger briefly described the ordeal to come. "It's two miles of pure fright. The water drops near thirty feet through rapids. Three of 'em, one after the other, all with rocks sharp as a bear's claw. Three channels through 'em, and Mike swears by the center but all depends on traffic. And a'course the weather." Enoch safely stowed his saddle and goods under a tarp in the cabin.

At Louisville, they did encounter traffic, but the skies were clear. On the docks, a number of flatboats waited for their turn or for a pilot with a crew experienced in running the rapids. Passengers and settlers disembarked, driving their livestock and carrying their valuables, and walked the well-trodden path down the Falls to the landing two miles below. As the *Gullywhumper* skimmed past the flatboats in line, Fink countered a storm of protests from the crews with the words, "Ain't I Mike Fink, king of the keelboaters? Kings don't wait on peasants." He laughed uproariously.

As the *Gullywhumper* entered the central channel and advanced into the first series of rapids, Mike Fink, as the strongest man of the crew, took control of the rudder. He ordered Tugger to the cabin roof, where Tugger roped himself to the sail mast. The pole setters took their positions on either side of the cabin, all of them roped to the gunnels in case they were thrown overboard.

Enoch offered to assist Fink at the rudder or to take a pole himself, but Mike waved him aside with contempt. "Yer a passenger, ain't ye? Passengers shelter in the cabin. I got no use for a greenhorn."

"The hell with you!" Enoch shouted back, his stomach lurching as the deck seemed to drop beneath him. He scrambled to the cabin roof where he could at least see Death coming. Tugger threw him a rope, and he, too, tied himself to the mast. Over the roar of the thrashing water, Tugger sent well-practiced hand signals to Fink to keep the boat on course. The pole setters used their long poles to fend off the rocks as the *Gullywhumper* was flung perilously close. At the stern, Fink heaved against the rudder arm with a giant's strength, eyes fixed on Tugger above him.

Just as Enoch began to breathe again in the first brief respite between the rapids, he saw a mast above the rocks. As the *Gullywhumper* dropped into the channel of the second rapids, he saw that the mast was attached to a heavily laden flatboat, struggling to maintain its course through the rough water. Boxes and bales flew into the river as the boat rocked from side to side. He shouted a warning to Tugger, who had spied a possible passage around the flatboat and was frantically signaling to Fink to change course to port.

But Fink did not change course. Whatever was ahead must make way for the *Gullywhumper*. From his vantage point, clinging to the mast, Enoch's heart was in his mouth as the keelboat rushed ever faster upon the floundering flatboat. He saw despair in the upturned faces of the flatboat's crew. As one, they raced fore and flung their poles and their bodies onto the deck, bracing against the oncoming shock of impact.

The crew of the *Gullywhumper* ran aft to also fling themselves to the deck, except for the indomitable Mike Fink, who couldn't see the flatboat immediately in his path. On the cabin roof, Enoch and Tugger wrapped themselves around the sail mast, clinging to each other. With a great grinding of wood on wood, the bow of the *Gullywhumper* slammed into the flatboat's stern, shattering its rudder into splinters, as water poured through broken planks. The flatboat shuddered as the *Gullywhumper*'s bow came to rest atop its rear deck. The keelboat rode the flatboat, as though urging it on, through the center channel of the second rapids and plunging down the precipitous drop to and then through the third.

Both boats, still united, arrived in the calm waters at the foot of the Falls. Fink's crew used their poles to push the *Gullywhumper* free of the flatboat, hurrahing as the bow slid groaning off the flatboat and wholly back into the river. The flatboat's crew, cursing vehemently, set their poles to push the clumsy craft to shore before it was swamped. Passengers of the flatboat, scattered along the shore, frantically rescued what they could hook of their cargo as it bobbed by.

The flatboat's pilot, apoplectic with rage, shook both fists at the notorious Mike Fink. "You'll pay for this, you bastard! I'll set the law on you," he spluttered. "I'll sue for damages, and lost wages, and compensation, and reckless disregard and for anything else my lawyer claims in court."

"Without me, yer mishmashed, leaky wooden box would have drowned itself. Ye should thank me for gettin' ye through, ye poxy, sniveling shore-hugger." Mike Fink was unrepentant. His frenetic mind was busy inventing a gloriously uproarious boast: How his *Gullywhumper* had ridden the deck of a flatboat down the Falls of the Ohio with nary a scratch to boat or crew.

After a swift inspection of the new set of scrapes and gouges to the *Gullywhumper*'s bow, Tugger prudently suggested the crew hoist the patched sail and swiftly depart, leaving the flatboat's angry pilot, crew, and passengers to get on with their business.

The wind had freshened, filling the sail and pushing the *Gullywhumper* at a brisk pace down to Clarksville, where they paused long enough for a closer inspection of the bow and starboard. Tugger looked doubtful, but Fink pronounced the *Gullywhumper* sound enough. He returned to the deck with a keg of rum.

Clear skies continued through the following days. Enoch idled away the hours gazing at cloud formations or into the river at the mesmerizing shoals of bluegills, the monster catfish, sauger, trout, eels, and beds of freshwater mussels in the shallows. Sometimes, he asked Tugger for the names of fish he didn't know. Often, Tugger merely shrugged. Enoch lazily watched osprey diligently fish for their brood. No one living along the river need go hungry. He noted with interest the bald eagles' vast and untidy stick nests lodged in tall trees and laughed to think that here in these skies lived his new nation's symbolic bird. He saw the curl of smoke from chimneys and sometimes saw stumps set afire in the new fields. Often, a pair of bright blue eyes appeared unbidden, but always welcome.

One day, thinking of Daisy, he remembered why he had dimly remembered the French name "Bellevue" when he saw that name on the docks at Pittsburgh. When he was a boy during the War of Independence, his older cousin Barnabas, when on leave from his duties as a courier for Whitcomb's Rangers, had regaled his family with tales of his adventures. Those tales had formed his boyish dreams of becoming a soldier himself. In one of the most exciting, a French ferryman and trader named Bellevue and his kind Abenaki wife had helped Barny disarm a detachment of Hessians under a British lieutenant and sent them packing on their disabled gunboat. Was it surprising that the Bellevues had turned up in Pittsburgh? He recalled no mention of a small daughter. It was something he looked forward to asking Daisy. It did not occur to him that Daisy was somehow already fixed into his future.

It did occur to him that Daisy Bellevue was the cause of Mike Fink's open hostility. Enoch suspected that Fink's hard looks, his ugly jokes, and mean jibes were born of jealousy. He thought it absurd that a rough and rowdy man like Fink could imagine that a lady like Daisy would look at him twice.

At last, in early May, twenty-nine days since he made his deal with Mike Fink, the *Gullywhumper* docked at the wide, wooden landing at Fort Massac. A new American flag snapped in the fresh breeze over the Commandant's headquarters. The original French fort had been rebuilt during Washington's presidency in the campaign against united Indian tribes in the Northwest Territory. Enoch, who had served under the command of General "Mad" Anthony Wayne, had risen to the rank of captain. From this fort, he and his volunteers would travel overland on the Massac Road to Kaskaskia, the few miles more to Cahokia, and then by ferry across the Mississippi to St. Louis.

Eagerly, Enoch unloaded his belongings onto the dock. He shook hands with the pole setters, putting a coin in each calloused hand, and said a warm and grateful goodbye to Tugger, leaving two coins in his palm.

Enoch saw with satisfaction that the fort's gates had opened, and the Commandant, three men in frontier garb whom he recognized, and a number of men in civilian clothes whom he didn't, were striding purposefully towards the landing. "A greeting party," he thought.

Mike Fink had eyes only for his departing passenger. "Are ye handing out my coins? Time to pay up, Locke. Tis under the thirty days." He held out a demanding hand.

"I pay my debts, Fink," Enoch countered, taking the little pouch from his inner pocket and tossing it over.

As he shook out the silver coins, Mike Fink asked the question that had burned in his mind since the day of departure. "Who gave ye leave to kiss the hand of my betrothed?"

"Betrothed?" Enoch said in confusion. His eyes narrowed. "You don't have the dad-blamed gall to mean Miss Bellevue, do you?" He saw Fink gather himself, veins popping in his neck and his face turning beet red, his hands clenching. His crew read the signs and immediately formed a cordon around the two combatants. Fink stepped closer with a menacing smile, his arms outstretched. This brawling giant of a man wanted nothing more than to squeeze the breath out of his rival.

Enoch boldly stepped into the circle of those bear-like arms and smartly brought his right fist upwards to connect squarely with Mike Fink's jutting chin. As Fink's head snapped upward, Enoch followed his uppercut with a left cross into Fink's jaw. The man staggered, his heel caught Enoch's saddle, and, in a windmill of arms, he fell backwards onto his keister.

"Here's our chance, boys! Get him while he's on his arse," one of the civilians shouted, and he and his posse pushed through the pole setters' cordon and fell upon Mike Fink. The constable from Louisville, as he proved to be, pulled out hand irons, and while his posse wrestled with the strenuously resisting Mike Fink, he slapped them on his wrists.

He waved a warrant in his face. "Mike Fink, you may be a snappin' turtle and king of the keelboaters, but you're on your way to Louisville to face charges," the constable said smugly. "I'll relieve you of that pouch, Mike. It'll go a ways to pay court costs and damages."

Pulled to his feet, spitting venom and curses, Mike Fink struggled yet to kick his rival off his feet. "Ye've been a jinx from the minute I clapped eyes on ye. Ye be a cheat and ye fight unfair." Even mad with rage, Mike Fink had the presence of mind to turn to his crew and say directly to Tugger, "Take care ye pole the *Gullywhumper* back to Louisville. I'll pick her up there."

Enoch had never been so relieved to see the back of a man as he was when the constable and his posse hustled Mike Fink mercifully out of hearing. Nor had he ever been so glad to see three men, trusted friends and fellow soldiers, even though they grinned like monkeys at him.

"Captain Locke, do you forget military etiquette?" Commandant Zebulon Pike, Sr. inquired sternly. All four soldiers snapped to attention and saluted the commanding officer.

FIVE

AT THE WATERING HOLE

"Take the gray, Husband. He needs to earn a name," Juniper urged Barnabas. "Tries Hard will serve well as your packhorse and relief mount." She turned to pat Tries Hard, who had fallen in behind them. The dog Cuervo trotted importantly ahead. It was dusk in the horse pasture where they talked quietly together on the eve of Barnabas's departure. Juniper continued. "By the time you return from St. Louis, we will all be in summer camp. A shorter distance for you to travel back to us."

"I don't like to leave you and Sky when everything is unsettled. I rely on Squando too much." But Barnabas was eager to assure his wife and himself that his reasons for going were sound. "We need powder and lead to defend our people. Parts, too, if they can be gotten, for the Charleville muskets we took from the French dead. Joshua Jones will have news, if there is any, of this new advance. Nothing happens along the Mississippi that he don't know.

And it will be well if my white face is not seen for a time." Here a touch of bitterness crept into his voice. "High Winds said out loud what others have kept quiet. It is better I am not part of the councils although, I lay odds, I will be welcome enough when I return with kegs of gunpowder."

Cuervo was sent to bring in the gray horse, who had been drifting towards them. The dog enjoyed the errand, expertly dodging a half-hearted kick, and the entire party returned in harmony to the village. The two horses went willingly into Little Bay's small enclosure, where the elderly horse greeted them with soft nickers. Barnabas paused to stroke his gray nose and softly spoke into his ear in American.

For most of the village youth, Little Bay's broad and patient back had been the first their little legs had straddled. One or another was often at his open gate to stroke his graying face and to bring him a handful of choice grass in friendship. At night, Barnabas wanted the old horse safely close by, and Little Bay increasingly chose to dream away his days in his own shelter.

Barnabas left before the sun was over the mountains. Squando rode with him for several miles, reminding him of the names of the Osage people who had taken him in when he was desperately wounded. He schooled him in the polite Osage words of greeting and thanks. "Forever my teacher," Barnabas nearly said aloud. Juniper had packed a number of carefully considered gifts of thanks should her husband encounter any of the Osage as he passed through their territory. In truth, Barnabas was glad enough to bid goodbye to wife and daughter, to his oldest friend, to the demands of village life, and to sternly command "Home" to Cuervo, who had trailed them without permission. He needed to be alone.

In parting, Squando lifted his hand to signify he had something important to say. "Barny, I had a vision after my arrow failed against LeBlanc. I saw him clearly raising a sword against you. I have thought hard and long on this. My visions are never clear about death. I believe it means that our failure to stop him was to be." Barnabas wondered yet again why Squando always had visions of him in danger.

The gray had nice gaits—a steady walk, an easy trot, an untiring lope. His ears swiveled backwards to catch the sound of Barnabas's voice, and his body promptly answered the commands of hands and legs. He got along companionably with Tries Hard. Proud of Juniper's good judgment of horses, Barnabas readily acknowledged that the gray was worthy of his respect. Only time would tell if he was worthy of his trust.

As he dropped out of the foothills and onto the plains, his spirits lightened under the broad sky and limitless horizon of new grass, colored in bright patches of spring flowers. He listened to the frenzy of birdsong, the sweet melody of larks, the jaunty voice of the black and white bobolink, the chuckling of prairie chickens rustling in the grass. The horses' hooves stirred up swarms of newly hatched grasshoppers, singing stridently. The shadows of large flocks in passage swept over the grasslands. Juniper had tried to teach him the Ute names of birds and small creatures, but he always set her laughing when he got them wrong. His keen hunter's eye focused on mule deer, antelope, elk, and the slowly moving herds of grazing buffalo with this year's red calves; but he was well provisioned, and his Jaeger stayed snug in its elk hide cover tethered to his saddle.

Days passed under a hot sun and nights under blazing stars. The cool wind seemed to blow his mind clear of the tumult of emotions that had besieged him for many months. His horses were company enough.

Paradise never lasts long. He had crossed from Ute to Arapaho and into Osage territory but had not encountered any of that tribe of fierce, warlike giants to whom he was beholden for his life. As he neared the watering hole, a swale where all travelers peaceably watered and rested their horses, he heard the unmistakeable report of a rifle shot. Barnabas was sorely disappointed; he had looked forward to lingering in this pleasant swale, shaded by cottonwoods and blessed with a pool of sweet spring water. His first instinct was to ride away and leave trouble to others.

Despite his better judgment, he nudged the gray closer to a point where he was clearly visible and lifted his covered rifle above his head to show his peaceful intentions. He heard the twang of loud American voices and spotted four white men with rifles, all pointed at nine Osage warriors, who were pointing their rifles at the white men. The Osage had spread out to make a perimeter on the grasslands. He noted with relief that they were not wearing black war paint. Likely, they were a hunting party aiming for the watering hole just as he had been. The white men were flouting the etiquette of the plains by aggressively blocking access to a watering spot used by all travelers but within the acknowledged territory of the Osage.

One brave, unarmed man stood on the lip of the swale between both parties, apparently attempting a negotiation. Barnabas recognized him as a Kansa known as Charley Potatoes, who was sometimes employed by Joshua Jones as a scout and guide across the grasslands from St. Louis. His wife, Barnabas remembered, was an Osage woman widely known for her excellent garden produce.

He walked his horses slowly, allowing for a cooling down of tempers as all eyes watched him.

He joined Charley Potatoes in his exposed position. To the Osage, in hand talk, he signed that he was the White Arapaho Man coming in peace. Remembering Squando's tutelage, he called out a greeting in their language. They conferred among themselves before signaling a greeting back to him.

"Hello, Charlie," Barnabas greeted the scout. "Can I be of help?"

"I am glad to see you, White Arapaho Man. One of these crazy white men shot at one of my relatives. May have put a bullet through his hair. Right about now everyone wants to shoot each other."

Barnabas looked down at the four white men pointing very good rifles at him. They looked military, acted like military men, and smelled like military men even in their frontier buckskins. Barnabas had been a military man himself and recognized his own kind. The military man in charge walked up the gentle slope to join his guide. One of the Osage rode within speaking distance and greeted Barnabas by name in hand talk. "White Arapaho Man, it is good to see you well." Barnabas was satisfied that all parties to the dispute were now in parley.

Enoch Locke saw that his guide, this somehow familiar stranger, and these very tall Indians all recognized one another. He felt on the defensive. Sensibly, he decided to adopt a conciliatory tone.

His mission was not to shoot Indians. He motioned to his men to lower their rifles. Then he spied the distinctive tomahawk on the wiry stranger's hip, and startled into quick anger, he hurled a harsh accusation. "Did you kill my cousin for his tomahawk?"

Barnabas's right hand settled immediately onto the handle of his 'hawk carried on his right hip, as much a part of himself as the hand itself. He looked down at the tomahawk carried on his accuser's hip, like a mirror image of his own. He swiftly retorted, "And how did you come by *my* cousin's 'hawk, did you kill *him* for it!"

Charley Potatoes intervened in disgust. "Tomahawks not important. Angry people make more trouble." The Osage watched with interest the family dispute between these two white men. The spokesman's mind at present was on compensation for the bloodied head of his comrade and the even more serious affront to Osage honor. He spoke in the voice of authority, accompanying his words with hand talk.

"Charley Potatoes, you tell these white men they are trespassing on Osage land. They drink our water. They fire at us without reason. They injure my sister's husband." Here the man turned to his relative, who raised a bloodstained hand from his head for all to see. "They insult us to our faces. I hold no grudge against the White Arapaho Man, who follows the people's way. I think these white men are far from home and should go back home. But they must pay restitution first."

Charley Potatoes interpreted the gist of this demand to both Barnabas and Enoch. "This Osage is plenty mad and wants payment. Show him what you have that makes him less mad."

"Bring up that canvas sack, Logan," Enoch ordered his corporal. Here was his chance to unload that heavy sack of moccasins his brother had foisted on him. But when Logan threw back the tarp, eight little brass-banded kegs of gunpowder were exposed. The Osage's eyes brightened, and a murmur of approval swept through his warriors. Barnabas was also suddenly very interested in the cargo these white men were carrying.

Logan brought up the sack, untied it, and tumbled the moccasins onto the open space before the Osage. The stern warriors chuckled. The Osage spokesman swung off his horse in one motion. He snatched up a pair of moccasins, compared it with the breadth and length of the moccasin on his foot, and held it up in scorn to show his warriors. As one man, they shook their heads.

"These moccasins are too little for Osage feet. Even our women's feet. You show us something our women cannot make." He looked pointedly at the tempting row of powder kegs.

Following that gaze and cursing his corporal under his breath, Enoch refused, with a sweeping gesture of dismissal, "Not even one keg." Barnabas looked thoughtful. Charley Potatoes did not need to interpret as a deep frown crossed the stern face of the Osage spokesman. Suddenly, the two sparring parties were again openly at odds and rifles were clenched tighter.

Charley Potatoes encouraged Enoch, "Offer one keg. A cheap price for all lives. Not good to make Osage enemies."

Enoch stubbornly shook his head, and the Osage spokesman raised three fingers and shook them in his face. He had remounted, and his warriors moved their horses closer to his. Intimidation was a useful weapon to use against whites.

Barnabas spoke up equably. "If you want to live, tell him one keg and all their horns filled with powder from another." He made the plus sign and said, "Two bars of lead." He looked towards Enoch for confirmation that lead was, in fact, available. Enoch nodded curtly.

Charley Potatoes officially made the offer, and it was accepted with a show of reluctance. Logan, to his chagrin, was dispatched to hand over one of the precious kegs, as well as two bars of lead and a handful of flints. "For God's sake, don't show anything else to these extortionists," Enoch growled.

Barnabas took it upon himself to fill each of the powder horns to the top. At the same time, he offered each warrior one of Juniper's small thank you gifts—finely worked, small deerskin pouches, each holding a brilliant quartz stone flecked with gold. The Utes held quartz to be of spiritual value. The powder the Osage accepted as their due; the pouches they acknowledged as thank you gifts from the White Arapaho Man's Ute wife.

The Osage consented to await the departure of the white men from the watering hole before they watered their thirsty horses. Charley Potatoes announced that he was handing his party of troublesome white men over to the White Arapaho Man. He spoke their language and was willing to take them on, one of them obviously blood kin.

Down in the cottonwoods, while Enoch's men quickly readied for departure, the cousins looked the other up and down, recognizing the Locke image in the other man. "He's more like me than like Ned," Barnabas thought, "though taller and heavier. He puts me in mind of Pa." Enoch, too, reluctantly saw his resemblance to his older cousin.

"I suspect you are Barnabas Locke, my cousin," Enoch said with a sheepish grin to Barnabas. "Sorry I tried to trade away your moccasins." He held out his hand.

Barnabas grasped it firmly. "A long way to come to deliver moccasins. Can you give me a piece of paper and a pencil? I need to send a note to a fellow in St. Louis. Charley Potatoes knows him. I think you might, too."

Enoch smiled. "I had the honor of meeting your 'fellow in St. Louis.' He commissioned me to deliver certain supplies when I encountered you. He seemed to have no doubt that we would meet. Indeed, Mr. Jones has entrusted me with a letter for *you*." He rummaged in his side pouch and withdrew a paper sealed with heavy wax stamped with the name *J. Jones, Esq.* He handed it over to his kinsman and watched his cousin's face shift with passing emotions as he read the missive. His lips moved, forming the words but not pronouncing them.

"Barnabas, I recognized your cousin as a Locke. Fifty French soldiers not in uniform left New Orleans on or about 15 April headed to Santa Fe. The man LeBlanc is alive and among them. Am sending powder, lead, flints, and a mainspring and parts for your Jaeger. Have put them on your account."

Barnabas twice slowly read the short letter. It confirmed Ramon's information and that the wily old sergeant in St Louis understood the situation. Taking the pencil offered by Enoch, he scribbled the words "*Recieved with thanks.*" He refolded the paper to give to Charley Potatoes. He returned the pencil to Enoch.

"So, Cousin Enoch, we have a few hundred miles to talk about family. Tell me first off how my uncle and aunt fare."

"They thrive, Barny, and the farm with them. People come from far about in spring to see the apple trees in white bloom, in the fall to buy eating apples and cider. They're good keepers through winter. Pa sells grafts of the Roxbury Russets. He calls them "Elizabeth's Apples." Cheese does well, too. They added on and the house is two stories now, more than twice as big."

In this agreeable way, the two cousins talked freely of their families but said not a word on other matters.

SIX

THROUGH THE BACK DOOR

Everyone in Santa Fe had heard the rumors. For over a year, word of a massacre of French gold miners had trickled out of the San Juan Mountains. Utes, it was said, had killed hundreds of miners after great provocations and the miners' discovery of a vast seam of gold. Every trapper, hunter, and trader who heard the story embellished it with lurid details. Not one miner had emerged to tell the truth. No gold had left those mountains. The intriguing mystery was widely discussed.

Ruiz, accompanied by the mestizo tracker Dominguez, left Rancho Aguilar in the early morning hours. It was agreed to keep quiet the rancho's association with the French, although it could not remain a secret long. They joined the French force under the military command of Captain Auguste Rocher at an abandoned outpost on the road north. Here, corralled mules carried provisions in leather-bottomed bags, sturdy enough to carry the weight of gold ingots. Ruiz knew the place well; he had designated it as the meeting point. LeBlanc strode forward to greet him, immediately stressing the urgency of departure.

Ruiz had not hit it off with Captain Auguste Rocher, who did not come to greet him. The man was surly, tight-lipped, arrogant, and was plainly aggrieved by this posting to the other side of the world from the arena of battle and promotion. He resented being chosen because of the Spanish he spoke fluently. While his men had kicked their heels in idleness and dissipation in Santa Fe, Rocher had dealt with frustrating delays in obtaining necessary mules, fresh horses, and sufficient provisions for men and beasts. He had been infuriated by the defection of one of his Spanish-speaking soldiers into the arms of a local woman. The suave merchant, Ramon Flores, quick to make assurances, had been slow to deliver on them.

Ruiz detested the French captain. He found LeBlanc to be more amenable but no less reticent. The man said little about the earlier French expedition to mine gold intended to fund the new French government. He said nothing of how he had managed to escape the massacre. He offered no explanation for the unsightly scar on his forehead, although he fingered it often. His Spanish was little better than Ruiz's French. The three met under the broken roof of the outpost to discuss logistics, with Rocher interpreting as necessary.

"Signor Ruiz, what route do you recommend? And to what advantage?" Rocher inquired civilly enough. LeBlanc leaned in to hear the answer.

"Through the back door, Messieurs. Your purpose is already guessed. Lookouts will have been posted. Traveling north along the east range of the mountains, a force this size can be easily tracked and more likely attacked by Comancheros, Apaches, Kiowa, Arapaho. Any number of bandits. These good rifles and good horses are a magnet. Better to arrive unannounced from an unexpected direction."

"But more miles to cover, yes?" probed Captain Rocher. "Harder terrain, yes? More days to travel, yes?"

"Yes, Captain, but are your soldiers not trained for just such a campaign?" Ruiz countered with a slight lift of his eyebrows. He spat tobacco juice.

Conversation grew heated, hampered by failures in translation. In the end, Rocher conceded to Ruiz's recommendations. He had no experience of this wild, vast country and no wish to learn. LeBlanc concurred reluctantly, but was himself unsure of the best route—what rivers would be forded, what high passes through those formidable mountains could be taken, what hostiles would be encountered. His experience of this country, first formed nearly four years ago, had been traveling north up the Mississippi, west up the Missouri River, across tallgrass country, and south into the mountains, not north through this desert high country. The map he carried secretly was useless from this direction. Ruiz presented himself as knowledgeable and confident in his judgment. And he had been recommended by the helpful, if inefficient, Santa Fe merchant Ramon Flores.

From the old outpost, the French force fell into a two-by-two formation. The packtrain of loaded mules followed. The scout Dominguez, half-Apache, was already reconnoitering their course ahead. Ruiz brought his horse alongside LeBlanc, not because he wanted the man's company but to glean what information might drop from those tight lips. Four Spanish-speaking soldiers rode close behind. The expedition turned northwest in the high desert country, following in the path of Franciscan monks who had ventured this way in a futile effort to find the Spanish missions of California. They had returned, sick and defeated, to Santa Fe.

After recent rains, the thirsty earth was greening with spring bloom. Nights were still bitterly cold, but the sun warmed their faces. Ruiz made sure the interpreters spread word to be mindful of rattlesnakes basking on the heated rocks. Their venom was deadly. For several days, the force made excellent time on the marked trail without any incident more troublesome than a broken cinch. Then luck turned sour.

When a band of mounted and armed Apaches appeared on a rocky ridge, as though out of the earth itself, Dominguez and Ruiz rode up to parley with them. Dominguez had expected this confrontation and made his greetings with great respect. These were Jicarilla Apache, not so ferociously warlike as their southern cousins, the Mescalero Apache, but this small band radiated a chilling menace. Dominguez recognized most of them by sight, but his Apache mother was not of their clan.

"These men are passing through. They mean no harm." Dominguez assured their chief.

"They look like soldiers. They ride like soldiers. They do not wear the clothes of soldiers. What are they if they are not soldiers?" The chief questioned. Dominguez shrugged. The Apache resumed, "Soldiers or not soldiers, they travel on Jicarilla lands and must pay for permission."

Dominguez turned to Ruiz and conveyed the message. Then he interpreted Ruiz's offer to the chief.

"Six woolen blankets, woven by Navajos at Santa Fe. Best quality."

The chief was unimpressed. "We have good blankets. We trade with the Navajo. One mule and the goods it carries."

When Ruiz returned with this demand, Rocher was loud in denial, shaking his fist towards the negotiators on the ridge top.

"Oh, blankets are not good enough for these wretches. Not one mule, not one pack. I give nothing but blankets to these aborigines!" The Apaches watched impassively, then turned their horses and melted away.

Despite sentries posted on the mule train, that same night one leather bag packed with smoked meat was taken. The sentries reported they had seen and heard nothing. Rocher raged. It meant they must start shooting game in the territory of these inhospitable savages.

He doubled the sentries the following night. Yet in the morning, one mule was missing. The six sentries had no morning rations. Instead, they were ordered under threat to retrieve the missing mule. There were no tracks in this hard earth to follow, nor did the soldiers venture far. They caught up later in the day with two rabbits but no mule.

Two days later, a soldier eating his midday rations on a flat rock, was snakebitten above his boot. He was one of the Spanish speakers. Ruiz rushed to his aid, wrapping a tourniquet above the bite and lancing it with his knife. He squeezed blood from the wound, but the skin around the bite was already discoloring. The soldier looked into Ruiz's eyes and saw his fate written there. He fumbled through his vest pockets and pulled out a slip of paper.

"Here," he said, "send word of my death to my parish priest. If any gold falls to my share, send it to him." The man trusted Ruiz rather than his commanding officer to perform this duty.

"Get him back on his horse," Rocher ordered. "He can die there if he must."

Many years ago, as a young corporal serving in the army garrison posted at Santa Fe, Ruiz had acknowledged only once an ambition he had long nursed privately. He yearned to find the ancient city of gold rumored to be lost in the steep mountain country to the northwest. After a bloody battle, glad to find himself still alive, he had confided his dream to a young American frontiersman, who had been a soldier like himself. Now, half a lifetime later, in idle conversation, Dominguez revealed that the Utes kept secret the location of the lost city, deeming it to be sacred, and that the Utes were not to be crossed. It was possible that his chance had come, along with this troop of benighted, gold-seeking Frenchmen. The back door to their dreams could prove to be the back door to his own.

The soldiers grumbled, as soldiers do, about the provisions, the loss of yet another comrade, and the unexpected dangers of this harsh, unforgiving land. The mountains loomed alongside them with their promise of riches and reward, and yet they continued westward on this monotonous plain of scrub and spiny cactus. Water was rationed. Two of their best marksmen went with Dominguez to hunt game so there was at least fresh meat with their beans, flatbread, and coffee. They knew hostile eyes watched them, and any sentry caught sleeping was under pain of a lashing.

Aware of his soldiers' discontent and his own impatience, Rocher pressed Ruiz. "We pass many canyons that must surely lead into the high country. And yet we do not turn up them. Why is this so?"

"Most of them are dry box canyons, leading nowhere. Dominguez is scouting for a canyon with water and a route to the high mesa country. Let us be patient a few days more."

Eventually, Dominguez did return with a promising report after a long two-day scout up and down prospective canyons. "There is one—grassy and well-watered. Many game trails. The ground rises to a steep trail onto the mesa above." Here, Dominguez paused for a long moment. "But I warn you that the Ancient Ones used this canyon long before us. Their spirits are strong there. If we pass this way, we must water fast and touch nothing." He looked dubious even as he described the bountiful nature of the canyon.

Chewing a twist of tobacco, Ruiz pondered the matter. He did not dismiss as superstition the mestizo's warning. As a good Catholic, he wore a cross about his neck, trusting to his faith to combat any lingering spirits of a people long dead. He feared living Utes more. He had delayed their approach into the mountains as long as he dared. He reported to Rocher and LeBlanc the news that Dominguez had found their back door into the mountains.

"This canyon should serve our purpose well. Dominguez saw no sign of watchers. But there is a caveat. We are entering grounds sacred to the Utes. They forbid any trespass that might arouse the anger of the Ancient Ones. We must pass quickly and without disturbance onto the mesa country above."

"I was doubting your usefulness, Ruiz," Rocher said. "Too many delays. Too much ill luck. I advise you to remain useful." Ruiz heard the veiled threat in his tone. LeBlanc eagerly approved the decision although he was curious about the caveat.

"Surely, you do not fear the ghosts of ancient savages. The Utes I have good reason to fear." He tapped the raised scar on his face.

At Ruiz's insistence, Rocher addressed his soldiers with direct orders to remain in tight formation and to touch nothing once they entered the canyon.

"There is no gold there," he emphasized. "We stop only long enough to water our horses and mules and fill our canteens. No one strays, no one goes off alone, not even to piss."

The mood lightened. That same night, under a half moon and around their campfires, the soldiers burst spontaneously into a ragged but spirited rendition of "*The Marseilles*," followed by ribald drinking songs. In a rare moment of solidarity, Captain Rocher broke open a small keg of rum, which he had been guarding jealously. He had hoped to keep it for a celebration of success, but judged this the opportunity to restore his soldiers' loyalty to him. Happy and almost optimistic, the soldiers wrapped themselves in their Navajo blankets and fell into sleep. As night deepened, the four sentries on their watch grew heavy-lidded, their heads drooping over hands crossed on their muskets.

From the dark shadows among the rocks emerged the brazenly erect shadows of men. A few horses stamped their hooves, but no one was awake to heed them. A mule coughed. A silent, abrupt death came to each sentry in turn. Each man was taken from behind, his throat slit, and his body lowered to the ground. Four mules and many bags of provisions disappeared into the night.

"They took their opportunity before it was lost to their allies, the Utes," Dominguez said regretfully to Ruiz, as they watched the burial of the four sentries under stones.

Rocher accosted Ruiz. "This is *your* failure. *You* camped us here." He pointed a rigid finger at Dominguez and shouted, spit flying, "And this is the work of *your* people. You claim to be a scout, but you saw and heard nothing?"

"An Apache is not seen unless he chooses so. By day or night." Dominguez stalked away, mounted his horse, and sat impassively.

Rocher turned his anger onto LeBlanc. "*You* accepted this man Ruiz as guide. You allowed that incompetent Flores to saddle us with a guide as incompetent as himself." He hurled a litany of accusations against LeBlanc, Ruiz, Dominguez, and the absent Santa Fe merchant Flores. Not one of them cared a whit.

Few words were said to speed the souls of the sentries. Rocher ordered the soldiers mounted even before the last stone was laid. Thoroughly dispirited and sullen, the French force later that day entered the mouth of the canyon under Dominguez's direction. They trotted two-by-two up several grassy miles, noting the tracks of game and the rivulets of spring melt trickling down the sandstone walls. When Dominguez raised his hand to halt the force, there was a murmur of approval among the soldiers. At one hand lay a pool of clear water. Flat stones kept the spillover in check. They were given the order to dismount. One soldier collected the canteens for four soldiers, filling and returning them. Another two soldiers carried four canvas buckets to water the horses and mules, two animals drinking out of the same bucket. This

practice carried on down the line as the most effi-
cient way to satisfy all those thirsty throats.

Across from the pool, up a short slope, the wall
of the canyon opened into a long overhang. At one
side, an upright rock, the height of a tall man, stood
like a sentry. From top to bottom, a mysterious
symbol was carved deeply into its red stone, like
a rope, tight at its center, each loop uncoiling outward. With the irresistible impulse to leave a mark
of their passage, a few reckless soldiers handed over
the reins of their horses and pulled out folding knives to scratch their names into the red rock.

Seeing them scramble up the short slope to the
standing stone, Dominguez flew into a fury. "You
fools! You bring the wrath of the Ancient Ones
down on us all."

LeBlanc swarmed into their midst, cuffing the
ears of the offending solders and striking knives
from their hands. "Did you not hear your captain's
order, 'Touch nothing.' Are you deaf? Stupid?"

Some of the soldiers swore later that the sentry
stone itself shook with anger. Its coiled rope seemed to pulse as the ground around it trembled,
stones rattling down the canyon walls. Neighing
horses and braying mules scrabbled for footing.

"Mount up, you fools," ordered Rocher. "Can't
you feel an earthquake under your feet?

Led by Dominguez, they surged forward in single file up the narrowing trail. Loose rocks pelted

them. In a state of suppressed panic, they barely noticed the symbols carved into the sandstone walls or the cairn of stones in a small clearing. Only Ruiz, coming up the rear, bent down to read the inscription on the flat stone topping the cairn. He leaned closer and with his gloved hand, he brushed it clean. Startling words carved in English made him smile. "Henry, a good horse" and the date "1782."

"Ah," he said to himself, "Barnabas Locke came this way all those years ago. Yes, one of his pack-horses was named Enrique." His own horse was urging him to move on and catch up.

One by one, they scrambled up the steep game trail to the lip of the mesa above. The muleteers whipped the mules forward. On the mesa top, the unnerving tremors intensified. The captain passed down the order, "Stay away from the rim. Close formation. Eyes forward. Keep those mules in line."

What Ruiz had long hoped to discover lay hidden behind a thick screen of juniper.

SEVEN

———— ♦ ————

THE SECRET WATCHER

Singing Grass walked beside her eldest son to a favorite parting point as he left the village, each of them leading a horse. They said few words but felt deeply the comfort of each other's presence. During her son's growing years, Singing Grass had watched vigilantly for signs of the violence and jealousy that had plagued his dead father. Her grandmother had assured her when Growler's Cub was born that his father had been a different man in his youth, a lively prankster and joker. A terrible blow from a Pawnee war club to his head had nearly killed him, but he had survived as a changed man, growing ever more morose, angry, and unwelcome.

"Squando speaks of you only with pride, my Cub. He knows you will do honor to your family as you did after the cleansing. That time was hard for all us Nuche."

They had reached the shallow ford in the creek where many others before had parted with words of good luck and encouragement. She rested her hand on his shoulder and smiled into his eyes. He put one hand on hers and pressed lightly. Then he mounted and took the lead strap of the packhorse from her hand.

"I was still untried then. Now is my time to prove myself a warrior. Mother, I will come back to you after counting many coup." He grinned as he boasted and then kicked his horse into a gallop and with a great splashing of water, crossed the creek. Singing Grass laughed to hear his sharp war cry.

Growler's Cub headed with his two horses to the far southwestern ranges of Ute territory. Without voicing his own opinion, he thought it unlikely that the French force would approach from this direction. More likely, he thought, they would come directly up from the south. But eyes were needed everywhere, and he went where his elders sent him.

Excitement surged through his veins. He had never been so wholly on his own before. He had served as his father's companion on many of Squando's visitations at tribal councils, both among the Nuche nation and of neighboring tribes. Squando was invited to talk of his visions, to interpret, and to offer his respected opinions on trade and relations among the tribes, as well as with the French, the Spanish, and the Americans. Always, Squando counseled that the patterns of life were changing rapidly with or without the consent of the peoples of the land. In this little space in time, Growler's Cub intended to do his part to protect the Nuche way.

As well as his tomahawk and the osage bow which he had made under his father's instruction, he proudly carried a musket, one that he had scavenged from the heap of weapons collected after the deaths of the French miners. It was French-made, a Charleville according to his uncle Barnabas, who had fought in a white man's war. Everything on the gun was good except for the severely bent barrel. No one else wanted it, but he saw the possibility of making it a useful weapon. He secured a full powder horn, shot, and flint. He set about obtaining the necessary files, and after painting the favorite horse of a warrior on an elk hide in trade for them, he spent hours cutting the steel cleanly below the bend. He also adjusted the length of the stock to make the gun compact and easily carried. He was proud of his handiwork, especially when his uncle Barnabas praised his efforts. "You made what I would call a hand-cannon," he said appreciatively. "You can shoot lead balls or scatter shot, even pebbles if you like." The musket was tethered to the front roll of his saddle.

His horses, He Bites and Surefoot, had been trained by his aunt Juniper, who famously bred and trained horses according to their merits and their dispositions. She had warned him that He

Bites was not entirely cured of that vice, especially when startled, but never bit out of malice. The Cub should keep that in mind when working around him. He was fast and agile and rode comfortably, saddled or bareback. Growler's Cub particularly liked the horse because his smooth dun coat showed off painted symbols. A roan with a red mane and tail, Surefoot's name summed up the best of him. He never put a hoof wrong. He was agreeable and a good companion for He Bites, who had never bitten him.

If he were asked to sum up his own nature, the Cub thought with amusement, he would say, "I like to make things from anything that comes to hand—paint, wood, leather, colored stones, and now I've done the same with metal." He was turning the musket over in his hands when he had that thought.

The Cub had paused his little party of three on a high rim. One towering peak to the north stabbed the sky like a needle. An eagle circled above him, and in the gorge far below flowed the snaking River of Souls. As Squando had told him to expect, he spied the path, a thin ribbon across the river meadows. Here, he would cross at the ford, underwater but providing firm footing. He was on the Old Path, used by Utes for generations to travel back and forth to the buffalo hunting grounds on the plains. First, he had to get himself and his horses down the stony and steeply winding trail to the river bottom. He clicked twice, and the two horses began to pick their way. Halfway, small stones rolled down from above. Both horses became skittish. He pressed his knees against He Bites's ribs to reassure him. He Bites settled, but as they descended to within the sound of the swiftly flowing river, both horses spooked again, their ears flattened, and their tails lashed. The Cub, too, sensed a hostile presence.

As they rounded a bend, they found the trail mostly blocked by a deadfall of firs, uprooted from above and carried down in an avalanche. As they navigated cautiously over and around the deadfall, the Cub looked behind to see why Surefoot was crowding so closely. Horrified, he saw a tawny streak of mountain cat springing effortlessly from log to log with its eyes fixed on the packhorse. Too late, the Cub dropped the lead strap to give the horse his head. The mountain cat sprang atop Surefoot, digging its claws into the pack baskets rather than into horseflesh. In terror, Surefoot screamed, bucked, and whirled. Both cat and baskets flew off his back, the cat tumbling into the tangle of the deadfall. But the snarling cat was not defeated. A yellow blur, he leaped back to the topmost branch and then dropped onto Surefoot's back.

The Cub's hand-cannon belched smoke and lead. In the instant he fired and dropped the gun, the Cub brought his bow into his hand, stringing it from his saddle and notching an arrow almost instantaneously. As the smoke cleared, he saw the bloodied mountain cat clinging to Surefoot with his fangs at the horse's neck. He let loose the arrow, striking the cat in its heart. It fell dead to the ground.

The Cub flung himself off He Bites, grabbed Surefoot's lead strap, and got both frenzied horses under his control and beyond the deadfall. Singing the lullaby his mother sang to calm his little brothers, he soothed the terrified horses down the trail and onto the river meadow. He walked them in circles until their eyes stopped rolling and their heads drooped to the lush grass.

The Cub took the chance of leaving them for the time it took to run back up the trail to retrieve the willow baskets at the site of the ambush. He stood for a moment over the dead mountain cat, offering a prayer of gratitude to the Creator for keeping him from panicking. He dutifully thanked the cat, but less earnestly, for giving up its life. As he admired its size and the color of its coat, his fingers twitched to part that pelt from its bones and to make something beautiful from it. He carefully extracted his precious arrow, glad that the arrow hole in the chest and the bullet hole in the flank were precise and clean. Those marks were the proof of his skill. "Father," he thought, "I am grateful to you for teaching me the skills of a bowman. I can never match you, but I make you proud today."

Thanks to Juniper's training, Surefoot stood patiently as the Cub cleaned his wounds with water. None were deep but all had drawn blood. He rummaged in one of the baskets for medicines Singing Grass had wisely put there. He found a small, tightly woven basket, lined with pitch, that contained a salve his mother and his aunt often used. His mother's words echoed in his head, "What heals you will heal a horse."

He also found, to his great pleasure, a pouch containing the ingredients for mixing paint with water and a number of his favorite feathers and peeled willow sticks for applying those paints. He sent a blessing to his mother, already many sun-rises behind him. She had always praised the lively images of horses he painted on their tipis, but also reminded him to be grateful for his gifts.

After gathering wood for his fire, filling his water gourds, and watering the horses at the river, he hobbled them to graze. Carrying his tomahawk, some cordage, and Surefoot's long lead strap, he hurried back up the trail to the deadfall. He set about lashing together a crude, short travois and hauled the heavy weight of the dead cat onto it. Its great head, with staring eyes and bared fangs, flopped into the air. Respectfully, he lifted it back onto the travois.

It was a hard drag down the trail and through the deep meadow grass. Both horses lifted their heads in alarm, snorting their disapproval. The Cub dragged the travois in a wide berth around them and eased the strap off his shoulders with relief. He spent the last of the daylight hours skinning and fleshing the pelt and carving out the choicest bits of meat—but none of the organs as he had been taught. He speared his cuts and propped them close to the flames of his fire to safely blacken his dinner. He left most of the meat smoking above the fire overnight.

In the morning, he rubbed fresh salve onto Surefoot's wounds before carefully placing the pack baskets over a smoothed blanket. He rolled up the cat's pelt and strapped it on top. Although he shied, Surefoot accepted his passenger without objection. They forded the high river without incident and began the ascent on the other side of the gorge. When they arrived on the western rim, high mountain meadows, bright with spring flowers and dotted with aspen groves and stands of fir and spruce, lay before them. Patches of snow still whitened the shade of stone outcroppings. The Old Path stretched ahead. From this point onward, he had to use the silent bow to shoot his dinner, conceal his small fires, and never present his silhouette against the sky. The Cub became a secret watcher.

He saw no one. He heard nothing. No ring of shod hooves on stone; no reverberation of a gunshot. He saw no signs of passage—tracks, stamped out fires, wood gathered, horse droppings, disturbed ground. His hopes of personal glory faded as the days passed, and he feared he had missed the great confrontation. He could figure out no good reason for the French invaders to pass through this far to the west. But white men had odd ways. His uncle, whom his father called "Barny," proved this to be a fact. Even if he missed the battle, the Cub was satisfied that the pelt of the mountain cat would prove his valor on his watch.

He came across the scattered bones of elk and deer, who had not survived the winter, but had fed the wolves. The greening meadows provided lush pasture for the night graze. His eyes, trained since earliest childhood, found edible plants to forage. When he had eaten the last smoked cuts of meat from the mountain cat, his arrows brought down rabbits, ground squirrels, and grouse. He preferred small game, quick to skin and roast. He hoped to shoot a deer or antelope to feed him during the long watch after he arrived at the place his uncle had described to him.

"You will find stone ruins where the Ancient Ones lived and stored their grain. Go no closer on the mesa top than the first ruins that will shelter you, hide the horses, and provide a lookout point.

Always remember this is sacred ground. You take nothing away. You show respect. Burn sage to cleanse yourself." He had slapped the Cub on the back to show encouragement.

His father's advice was explicit. "Do not put yourself in danger. You watch. Report back when the moon is fat again if you have seen nothing. If you do see or hear anything that tells you the French are coming this way, then you ride to the foot of the Long Falling Water to report as fast as your horses will carry you."

He had moved nine beads on his counting cord when he arrived on the green mesa dotted with strange, unnatural places made of stone and falling into ruin. He had been taught that places where the Ancient Ones had lived were sacred and taboo. Their spirits dwelled there still. It was wise to leave them alone.

As his uncle had described, he found just such a ruin to serve as his watching post. The thick stone walls loomed high above his head and log beams still held most of the roof in place. He could perch up there and see for a distance. There was space enough to shelter both horses and himself. A little stream, full of spring melt and shielded by junipers and piñon trees, ran a short distance behind. Likely, the stream would go dry by midsummer. This ruin would do, but the Cub felt uneasy here, like a trespasser.

Perched on those walls, the Cub thought often of his puzzling uncle, a white man like these unseen French soldiers. Barnabas, he guessed, thought of himself as a blood brother to the Cub's Abenaki father, as part Arapaho by virtue of his initiation into their Red Circle warrior society, and part Ute by his marriage to his aunt Juniper. Yet he never pretended he wasn't a white man by birth and upbringing. Sky Feather spoke American when she was alone with her father; the Cub couldn't say if she spoke it well or not. Uncle Barnabas taught him and his little brothers lots of words in American. He said they would need to speak to white men sooner or later and might as well know enough to rub along.

His father always agreed. He would say, "Hand talk is useful in its way, but to know a man, you need to hear his voice saying the words. Trust is another thing." The Cub understood that his father expected him to learn and remember exactly the words that other people spoke when they traveled together to council fires.

Uncle Barnabas was acknowledged to be a good storyteller in his white man's fashion around the evening fire. Many of his most welcome stories were about his adventures as a ranger and scout for the American militia during their war with the English King. He spoke often of the bravery and loyalty of his horse, Little Bay. The Cub would look in wonder at the kind, grizzled old horse he had ridden when he was little more than a baby. His favorite stories were about the Bear Dog Amigo, Cuervo's grandsire. How he had bested a bear in a blueberry thicket, and rescued his uncle from a deep pit, and killed a wolf-dog in a fair fight, and counted coup on a bad Ute, whom his uncle would never name.

Once, when they were still children, Sky Feather asked her father about his American name. "Why does my Uncle Squando call you 'Barny?' What does it mean?"

Everyone around the fire paused to hear his answer. "It's the name he called me when we were boys. It's short for 'Barnabas.' My family's name is 'Locke.' I guess that has to do with locking things up to keep out thieves, but Utes aren't thieves, unless he's taking horses from somebody else." It was a diplomatic answer, not entirely true, but everyone laughed.

Sky Feather was still puzzled. She rolled the name "Barnabas" around in her mouth several times, but it did not suit. "Then what does 'Barnabas' mean, Father?" she asked.

Barnabas considered the question. Finally, he said in a mix of American and Ute, accompanying his words with hand talk, "As I recollect, Barnabas was a fellow in the white man's holy book. He took up with another holy man name of Paul, and they went west as partners to bring the word of God to the heathens. My Ma liked the sound of that name and liked to point it out to me when she taught me reading from the Bible."

When Sky Feather had thought this curious reply over, she asked, "You and Uncle Squando are like the holy men, but who are the heathens?" The children were told to go to sleep.

Yes, it was a hard fact that his uncle, although liked and widely respected, was a white man. It was his father, Squando, the Abenaki Prophet, who was taken into the Nuche as one of their own. Two springs ago, when a small band of the French miners affronted Ute women as their band traveled to the Bear Dance, his uncle and his father had hunted down and killed those nine men. But when the Utes across their territory rose up as one against the entire French expedition, Uncle Barnabas was visiting his Arapaho family and seeking out their famed medicine man Blue Smoke for healing ceremonies. Growler's Cub knew that some Utes said that his uncle could not war against the French, because they had been the allies of the Americans in their war against the English King, and because they were white men. His reputation among many Utes was tarnished. The Cub thought this was unfair.

Each day the Cub rode an early morning and a late afternoon circuit of the mesa. Sometimes he stopped to pick up a colorful stone or a hawk's feather to twine in his horses' manes, or to trace the passage of huge numbers of birds. While light lasted, he sometimes mixed his paints with water and painted on his horses's smooth coats strange symbols that he saw carved into ruined walls. On Surefoot, he painted a mountain lion.

Late in the morning of the fifteenth bead, after his morning patrol, he took the horses down to the stream for all of them to drink. Surefoot and He Bites became agitated and hung back on their leads. The water in the stream seemed to bubble and then to wash violently back and forth. Suddenly, the earth trembled and then shook and then rocked him nearly off his feet. The earth itself seemed to bellow in pain. Trees along the creek bed bent in half, shattering the trunks. Jagged cracks opened in the ground.

"Did I offend you?" he shouted to the Ancient Ones. "Are you angry with me?" And then in hope, "Or with someone else?"

He struggled to keep the long leads in his hands as both horses reared in terror and tried to rip free. Surefoot yanked away, stamping on the Cub's right foot in the confusion. He leaped over the little stream and galloped off beyond the wavering tree line. He Bites fought the Cub, desperate to follow. Curling his lip and snaking his head, he bared his long teeth and bit the Cub high on the arm holding his lead. The Cub yelped and let go. "No malice," he thought bitterly, clutching his right hand to his left shoulder and recalling his aunt's assurance.

Limping and staggering as the ground shifted under his feet, he hurried back as best he could to the ruin, not knowing where else to seek shelter. Crossing the threshold, he was almost amused to find both his panicked horses cowering in a corner under the broken roof. He cowered, too, as the tremors continued, gradually lessening in length and intensity. When finally the earth stood still, the Cub rose, badly shaken, and disentangled He Bites from the lead dragging under his hooves. He took him outside into the late sunlight.

"Your name does not give you the right to bite me. You hurt me!" The Cub pulled the offending nose down to his bitten shoulder and into a trickle of blood. He Bites jerked his head away, his eyes rolling. The Cub pulled his nose back again and rubbed it into the teeth marks on his skin.

"You don't like it. I don't like it. Never do that again," the Cub admonished and loosened his grip. He Bites lowered his head and sighed deeply.

Although his right foot and left shoulder throbbed with pain, he led his horses back to the stream. They all drank with a day's thirst. The horses behaved, and he forgave them. He had been just as scared. He said a prayer of fervent thanks to the Creator that they had not been swallowed into the angry earth.

Inside the ruin, the Cub retrieved the little basket containing the salve he had used to treat Surefoot's bite wounds. Those were healing cleanly. He dipped a finger into the salve and smeared it onto his shoulder. It was soothing and in a few moments numbed the pain. "Ah," he thought, remembering his mother's advice, "this salve does work for people." He removed his right moccasin and inspected the damage. He could wiggle his toes and flex the foot. There would be bruises, swelling, and pain. He dipped his finger again into the salve and gently rubbed it across the top of his foot. It could not hurt to try.

Mother Earth settled herself. Instinct urged the Cub to leave his post and to rendezvous at the Long Falling Water. For several nights, he watched the moon rounding, shedding more light, but not yet fat and full. On the sunrise of the twentieth bead, he determined to ride a last, larger perimeter of the mesa top. His eyes scoured the ground for signs of passage, and there, past a huge thicket of blueberry bushes, he found horse droppings. He dismounted and examined them closely. Crows and jays had scavenged them for seeds and scattered them. He followed a long line of droppings at least five days old. Hoofprints identified them as the droppings of horses and mules galloping in close columns. He sat back on his haunches thinking.

"They passed by me on the day Mother Earth shook. I have been waiting here like a fool." His eyes caught the gleam of a brass button in the dirt, and he laughed bitterly.

EIGHT

A VENGEFUL BULL

Barnabas hungered for news of his family in the distant East. When informed that his cousin Ned was a newly minted United States Senator, he laughed aloud. "I reckon it's no surprise. Ned had bigger ideas than being an apple farmer. I expect his wife, Lucy Forrester, takes just fine to that life." Enoch chuckled too.

Barnabas had other matters to ponder. "Why," he had wondered since their meeting in the Osage swale, "is Cousin Enoch appearing with a small detachment just now when the French are showing their faces? This is no hunting party. If Cousin Ned has sent Enoch here and Joshua Jones sends kegs of powder along with him, then Enoch has more to tell than he's saying." Those eight kegs weighed heavily on his mind. Obtaining them was the purpose of his journey to St. Louis. "Jones already guessed why I might come. Ramon Flores knows. So must Isabella. Two Rivers knows. Hell, Charley Potatoes probably knows."

Midmorning of the third day traveling together, the four men crested a rise and halted as one. Below and beyond, as far as their amazed eyes could see, buffalo by the thousands grazed in the windblown grass. Some rolled in dust wallows; cows nursed red calves; young bulls sparred. Old bulls guarded the perimeters, watchful for hunters—wolf packs or humans on horses. The stink and size and sounds of thousands of huffing, grunting, bawling, farting, stamping giants seized their senses and rendered them mute. Even after these many years in the tallgrass country, Barnabas was as astonished as the wide-eyed newcomers riding with him. Their mounts danced nervously beneath them, and the packhorses pulled back on their leads. The men immediately began to uncinch their rifles from their saddle horns. Barnabas raised a hand slowly and stopped them.

"One gunshot will send a panic through this herd. If they stampede in our direction, we are dead men. They will outrun us and swallow us."

Barnabas scanned the endless columns of behemoths in slow motion through the grass. He had never seen this massed number before, but had listened with awe to stories of hunting parties that had come upon these unmanageable gatherings and had postponed their hunt until the masses had broken apart into individual herds.

Barnabas briefly considered whether they could slip through those masses without creating alarm. He dismissed that notion. Buffalo had poor sight but keen hearing. The buffalo had already scented something amiss, all of them rising and standing alert.

"We move south without exposing ourselves. Your chance to use those fancy rifles will come another time. Buffalo hunting is dangerous even with seasoned ponies. Buffalo are unpredictable. We drop off this ridge out of sight and hearing and ride as quiet as we can until they pass."

His plan was sensible. Enoch cautioned his men. "In this country, we are new recruits. We know nothing. My cousin's strategy will save our lives so that we can complete . . ." Here he suddenly went silent. In his military mind, Barnabas heard the unspoken words, "our mission." "So," he thought, "Enoch knows about the gold."

The earth beneath them suddenly shuddered. Below them, the great herd surged outwards in all directions. Barnabas's first thought was that their presence had stampeded the buffalo, and that the earth trembled from their hooves. Now the whole earth distinctly shook. The ground itself was moving, and the buffalo were fleeing. A large number of them pounded up the long slope in their direction.

"Follow me. We ride to the river and across. Let go the packhorses. Ride for your life!" Barnabas shouted, wheeling the gray horse about.

In this instant of decision, he thought of the river called the Smokey some miles to the south. If they got across its banks first, the herd might slow down there and stop to drink and to get the calves safely across. He had seen for himself how long and how fast buffalo could tear across the tallgrass. If the ground didn't shake apart, they still had a chance.

Terrified, the horses, mounted or carrying packs, ran flat out. Their riders leaned forward, taking their weight off the horses's backs, clinging with their knees. Soon, buffalo passed them on either side, and the riders were lost from sight of one another. The shifting ground beneath the hooves tripped some buffalo to their knees, but they staggered, rose, and ran on, ignoring the horsemen and their packhorses now in their midst. Man or animal, everyone was racing for their own lives.

The gray horse needed no urging. Barnabas began to believe that, if a prairie dog hole didn't trip the gray, they might escape by the skin of their teeth. The horse beneath him matched eye for beady eye the buffalo as they lumbered at racing speed beside and then beyond them.

Barnabas choked in the dust and stink of the buffaloes surging around him. He was grateful that he rode a Ute saddle, not the heavy military saddles of his cousin's detachment. Every ounce of weight slowed a horse. Gradually, the number of buffaloes thinned. They had outpaced even the gray horse, who had won races under Juniper. He gently tugged the gray into a gallop, enough speed to keep them from being overrun by the cows with calves but not fast enough to burst a horse's heart.

Out of the corner of his eye, he saw another horse galloping just behind the gray. With relief, he recognized Tries Hard. Though lathered and covered in dust, he still carried his packs. Barnabas was glad not to have to report his demise to Juniper, who valued this sensible and useful animal.

The horses sensed the river before he did. His nose was packed with dirt and buffalo stink. Only stragglers now passed, plunging off the churned-up river bank into the water and across. Barnabas slowed the gray to a walk, and Tries Hard fell in behind. Both horses were blowing hard, ribs heaving and red nostrils distended. As they slid down the muddy bank of the Smokey, they tried to drink but Barnabas forced them forward out of the roiled, unclean water. Bodies of the young and unwary floated in the current.

Safely on the other side, Barnabas wiped his streaming eyes and snorted out the snot from his clogged nostrils. He smelled smoke and his hopes rose. Only a few hundred yards upstream, above a cluster of cottonwoods, he spied a column of smoke and, if his eyes were to be trusted, a horse among the trees.

"Hallooo," he called and urged the gray horse forward. Instead, as though sprung out of the ground, an old and battle-scarred graybeard of a buffalo bull, chuffing in anger, confronted him. The bull's club-like tail was stiffly raised. His eyes fixed on the gray horse. Sensibly, Tries Hard whirled about and departed. The gray horse stood his ground.

"Good God," Barnabas whispered in horror. When the bull charged, the gray horse danced aside, and the bull passed. It spun around and renewed its charge. As its lowered head tilted to rake the horse with the wicked curve of his horn, the gray horse again nimbly danced away. Then he whirled and launched a kick with both hooves into the bull's ribs. Barnabas flew over his head and landed on his back with a thump that drove the air from his lungs. The bull bellowed, swung again his mighty head, and again the gray kicked, this time strategically at the bull's rear legs. The bull stumbled, rose, and stood thinking for a long moment. The massive head turned slowly, changing its focus from the horse to the man on the ground only yards away.

Barnabas had half risen and saw the monster fixing its angry eye upon him. His body rose of its own volition and propelled him towards the trees. The bull fell in behind him. In a few more steps, he would charge this interloper. But the gray horse had not finished with his opponent. He trotted between his rider and the bull, and as the bull charged in vexation, the horse reared high and came down with his front hooves smashing into the bull's snout, whirling and landing another kick. In fury and pain, the bull returned his attention to the horse and launched his enormous weight against him. The agile gray yet again sidestepped the charge.

From the cottonwoods, a rifle cracked. The bull shook his massive head, his legs slowly buckled, and he collapsed like a small hill falling. With a quiver of ancient flesh, the spirit passed from him. A figure jumped down from a cottonwood limb and raced toward Barnabas, flinging an arm around his sagging shoulder. It was Sergeant McFee, still clutching his Springfield and babbling in a burst of spent nerves.

"I couldn't get a bead on the bull. You or the horse was always in the way. That damn bull chased me up a tree, and I swear he was going to shake me out of it. He heard you cross the river and fixed on you to kill instead. I jumped down for my rifle and back up to get a heart shot. That gray horse of yours . . . I've never seen anything like him. Are all Indian ponies as brave as that?"

Barnabas felt that the gray had earned his name. He turned to the horse, taking his head into his arms and breathing into a cocked ear, "You are Stands His Ground. You are as brave as any horse I ever rode." As those words passed his lips and entered the soul of the horse before him, Barnabas was shaken by a wave of sadness, of loss, of grief.

Tries Hard returned unrepentant. Stands His Ground nickered a friendly greeting. Barnabas and the marksman Sergeant Patrick McFee piled rotting wood onto the fire, so that smoke billowed upward as a signal. They waited as the day passed and the earth settled back into herself, both desperately hoping for the safe arrival of the others. A weary Sergeant Thomas Crisp found them, dropping off his exhausted horse and hugging his fellow sergeant in profound relief.

He looked about and asked, "Where's the captain? Where's Logan?" He was answered with glum silence. Hours later, Enoch rode into the cottonwood grove with two packhorses behind him. "These two didn't make it easy. But here they are, powder kegs intact." The cousins nodded to one another.

"I thought I lost you. I thought I lost all of you," Enoch said, quickly followed by, "Where's Corporal Logan?"

Enoch decided they would fan out at first light and go back to look for their lost comrade. Barnabas did not object, although he had little hope Logan would be found. Yet, the man deserved the respect of an attempted rescue. Each of them took a turn to keep the fire burning brightly through the night, but Corporal Daniel Logan did not ride into camp. Hopes rose only to be replaced with dread as straggling buffalo came down to the river to drink. Beyond the firelight, they moved like darker shadows in the darkness, huffing and belching. Huddled in the cottonwoods, the men felt encircled by enemies.

At first light, with the fire smoldering to ashes, the party rose, each man aching in body and morose in spirit. The horses alerted them, and they stood well back in the cottonwoods as a line of strange, humpbacked mourners filed to the spot where the old patriarch lay. Cows and young bulls circled the corpse with lowered heads, each taking it in turn to nudge the still body back into life. Respectfully, they chuffed a mumbling farewell. The ceremony complete, they departed as formally as they had come in a single line.

To Enoch, Barnabas said in a low murmur, "A very old Arapaho friend—his name was Young Raven—told the story of a fallen bull mourned by his family. I thought it was an old man's fancy, but now I seen it with my own eyes."

They did not find Corporal Daniel Logan. They did find the trampled body of his horse, and the captain removed the Springfield Armory rifle from the saddle. They stood together near the dead horse and offered a military salute to the departed soul of their fellow soldier. Sergeant McFee began to whistle a jaunty marching tune played in army camps. Captain Locke, Sergeant Crisp and ex-Corporal Barnabas Locke joined in whistling "Yankee Doodle Dandy." The captain said a brief prayer. They could do no more. In battle, it was often so.

NINE

TALK AT THE ARAPAHO VILLAGE

The ground had shaken hard in the Arapaho village. Women had already mended damage done to their lodges. Old people had not been surprised, although what it portended was a mystery. "Who has angered Mother Earth?" was the question on everyone's lips.

One old jokester quipped, "Mother Earth is farting." A few laughed; others looked askance. "Ah," predicted one old widow woman, "someone is coming."

She was right. Three days later, youths rode into the village to announce, "White Arapaho Man comes. Three yellow-hides ride with him. They have long guns." Already uneasy, the village took precautions. Women directed small children and girls into the safety of the secret dugouts hidden in the willow thickets along the creek bank. Youths were sent to alert the warriors, Two Rivers among them, patrolling southern boundaries. Old men, who had aged out of the Red Circle warrior society, stepped forward to greet their fellow member and friend, who arrived with a party of whites from the north.

"You are welcome, White Arapaho Man," greeted the senior elder, Sharp Nose, a man still erect and impressive in his old age. He and his cohorts waited patiently as Barnabas and his party dismounted and as Barnabas introduced his blood kin and his cousin's two friends. At Sharp Nose's signal, boys darted forward to take the reins of the weary horses and led them away to strip them of saddles and packs, to water and turn them out into the horse pasture. Other boys were sent to prepare the fire and bring water for a cleansing sweat in the sweat lodge. Women hustled to the cook fires to add more meat to the stewpots.

"They say they come to hunt buffalo, Sharp Nose, but the buffalo hunted us. We were caught in their midst when the earth shook and the buffalo stampeded. I have seen buffalo by the many hundreds, but these were beyond counting. My kinsman," and Barnabas nodded towards Enoch, "invited old comrades to join him in a great adventure. One of them paid for his adventure with his life." All this was said in Arapaho, Barnabas emphasizing his words with hand talk. "That other matter is none of their business."

Sharp Nose understood his private meaning. Generously, he offered the hospitality of the village, inviting Barnabas into his own lodge. Quarters were found for the three visitors, and all were warmly welcomed by their hosts. Nothing was said of the threat posed by French soldiers seeking gold.

Barnabas was in a quandary. It was imperative to deliver those kegs of powder into the hands of Squando, Buffalo Bones and Walking Man, the leaders of those who supported his plan to defeat the French. Here among the friendly Arapaho, Enoch and his comrades were safe under his protection, whether they knew it or not. Among the Utes, three more yellow-hides would not be welcome. Their gold fever was known to be incurable. Barnabas was bitterly aware that even he was under suspicion, fanned by his old adversary High Winds.

It was a tangled knot, difficult to unpick. To do so, he and Enoch needed to come to a frank understanding. He invited Enoch to ride out alone with him into the tallgrass towards the Sun Mountain, its snowy peak shining in the distance.

"My wife, Juniper, belongs to the band of Ute people who call themselves "People of Sun Mountain." Its Ute name is "Tava," and it is the holy place where all Utes were created. My Arapaho people call it Long Mountain, and they respect the Utes' claim to that region. I first met my Ute family in its shadow. I reckon it's sacred to me." He signaled Stands His Ground to halt and turned in his Ute saddle to Enoch.

"You are not here to deliver moccasins or to swap family news with a lost kinsman or to hunt buffalo. Tell me your mission, Captain Locke, and I will tell you mine."

Enoch considered. He had seen for himself the vast distances of this country, its dangers, and that the native peoples ruled here. His mission was doomed without the guidance of this familiar but puzzling cousin.

"Ned—not as your cousin or my brother—but Senator Edward Locke, Jr. sent me to you under military orders. Yes, I hold the rank of captain and Crisp and McFee are sergeants acting under my orders. Those orders are to determine whether rumors are true of a French expedition dispatched to the San Juan mountains in Indian territory to retrieve a fortune in gold. In St. Louis, I learned that those rumors *are* true. My mission henceforward is to locate that gold and to track it, probably to New Orleans, maybe coming down the Arkansas River. My mission is to stop that gold, enough to fund the new French government teetering on bankruptcy, from leaving our territorial waters. We are a step away from being on a war footing, Barny, with our old wartime ally. It would be a triumph for both Senator Locke and his humble brother if that gold is recovered by the United States government rather than by the French, or the Spanish come to that. So, yes, Barny, I have a bigger stake in this adventure than delivering moccasins."

Deep in thought, Barnabas eventually replied. "My mission is to keep that gold from ever leaving the mountains. If word gets out, Ute territory will be overrun by white men seeking gold. Enoch, I saw it happen myself and the end of that story was death to hundreds of mining men. Only the story didn't end there, and I must take the blame for that. I let one man escape, and that man has returned with others. Gold is a curse to the Utes, a shiny stone without value."

"How will the French now in Ute territory escape with the gold, Barny? The powder Mr. Jones sent to you, in my care I admit, is intended to arm the Utes, not the French. I don't ask you to support my cause, only to not impede it. Can you do that for the American government, if not for me and Ned?"

Again, Barnabas sank into thought before replying, "I reckon, I can't, Enoch. No promises I can't keep. One thing for sure is that you and your sergeants will not be entering Ute territory."

They turned back to the village as cousins but not allies. On their return, they found more surprise visitors awaiting them. Juniper strode towards them, her figure tall and supple in her fringed buckskin dress, her thick black hair rippling over her shoulders. Always, the sight of her lifted her husband's spirits, never more so than now.

She stopped before them, startled. Her gaze traveled from face to face and back again more slowly. "Husband, who is this strange-looking man?" she said with a straight face but with laughter in her eyes. They took to each other, Enoch and his cousin's Ute wife, from that moment of meeting.

Sky Feather stepped forward and greeted her father's cousin in bold American, "Hello, my father's kinsman. Do you have a wife? Do you have sons and daughters? How old are they? Do you keep many horses?"

"Later, later, Sky, you can ask questions later," Barnabas laughed indulgently. He almost pitied his cousin for the barrage of questions that would come from his daughter.

Enoch extended his hand to Sky Feather. She shook it with a firm grasp. "I am pleased to meet you, Miss Sky. I am impressed by your good English."

She tossed her head and replied confidently, "Oh, that is nothing. I speak American and some French and Spanish, Arapaho and Ute of course, and hand talk when we meet with other peoples of the tallgrass country. Father says I will need to speak with white people sooner or later and now," and she laughed, "sooner has come."

Then Cuervo insisted on being introduced, rising to his full height and placing his front paws on Enoch's shoulders to look at him face to face. Enoch was nearly staggered backwards by the dog's vehemence. Enoch scratched that sweet spot behind Cuervo's ears and thumped his ribs. Man and dog approved of one another. The dog dropped on command to his haunches, his long tail whipping through the grass.

Singing Grass and her two young sons accompanied Juniper. Barnabas introduced her to Enoch with great ceremony. Singing Grass was warm in her sweet, shy way, but the boys were eager to show off their American. "Hello, glad to meet you," they shouted and solemnly shook the white hand extended to them.

They walked as a happy family party into the village, where two tipis were being raised by many cheerful hands. Juniper had brought, as was her practice when visiting, three well-broken young horses that she judged ready for further training by new owners. Her reputation as a horsewoman was high among all the neighboring tribes, some calling her with great respect "Horse Medicine Woman." Her advice was sought to cure both bad habits and bad injuries.

Looking over the horses that had traveled with his family, Barnabas felt as though a shadow had fallen over him. He looked at Juniper, and she shook her head, pulling him away. As they walked under the cottonwoods together, she answered his unasked question, steadying her emotions before she spoke.

"Cuervo found him at the top of the horse pasture and came for me. He was lying peacefully next to the pile of stones where Amigo lies. It was late on the day when Mother Earth shook. After sunrise, everyone came up to dig his grave and lay him beneath the stones you had ready for him. Children lined his grave with sweetgrass and sage. He was buried with the honors due a warhorse to the sound of drumming. We chanted the Song to the Horse as his spirit galloped away, one singer after another repeating the song." Juniper put her hand into her husband's and slid from her wrist onto his a closely woven circle of dark horsehair.

"Here, Husband, you will carry this token of Little Bay wherever you are. His spirit will remain strong with you."

Barnabas drew her closer, raising her hand and kissing her calloused palm. "The gray horse has earned his name, Juniper. He saved my life late on the day Mother Earth shook. His name is 'Stands His Ground.' At the moment I told the gray his name, I felt the passing of another horse." They walked quietly back into the village. "Oh," he said, almost as a reminder to himself, "be nice to Sergeant Patrick McFee. He's a damn good shot."

Many people had much to say as they passed between the two Ute tipis that evening. Barnabas and Sky Feather interpreted. Everyone appreciated the individual stories told by the four survivors of the Great Buffalo Stampede. Barnabas invited Patrick McFee to tell, from his point of view perched in the cottonwood tree, the story of the battle between Stands His Ground and the venerable old bull. McFee proved to be a gifted storyteller, employing his own dramatic gestures to paint the picture for his listeners. Barnabas commended him for his excellent marksmanship and then tapped Enoch to relay the story of the death ceremony held over the body of the fallen patriarch. Sharp Nose, his pipe forgotten in his lap, confirmed that he had seen this ritual in his youth with the much older and greatly revered warrior Young Raven.

After the two sergeants made their good nights and the Arapaho guests at length departed, Sky Feather seized her opportunity to quiz her cousin Enoch on the life of her American family, with special curiosity about girls of her age. What did they wear? Did they ride? Did they dance, sing, run? Did they go to school? What did they learn? Did they choose their husbands? Her questions were pertinent and probing, although she had to turn to her father for certain words.

"Someday, I will see for myself how Americans live far to the east of the Great River," she said with a confidence that made her parents uneasy. She was fourteen and already was charting her future. Juniper rose and bid Sky Feather accompany her for the end-of-the-day check on the horses. She invited Enoch to join them, and only Barnabas and Singing Grass were left in the tipi to hear Sky Feather's eager young voice launching another volley of questions.

"She comes of age so quickly. But there is no holding them back. My Cub is far away from me doing a man's duty. Barny, I am glad of this quiet moment to tell you things that my absent husband wishes you to know." Singing Grass composed her thoughts, raising a hand to signal their importance, just as her husband did. Barnabas understood the unconscious gesture.

"Visions descend upon my husband that disturb his peace. Barny, he foresaw that Mother Earth would make her anger known, that uncountable numbers of buffalo would race across the tallgrass and then disappear; he fears forever. He sees whirling winds take up men and swallow them. He sees images of dangers to those he loves. Somehow, the man LeBlanc is at the heart of these evils, but my husband can make no clear picture of them. He is sure only that you are in danger and must not return into the mountains until the French are dead or gone. He knew I would find you here. Barny, my husband bids me to bring the powder to the meeting place at the Long Falling Water. Sharp Nose will accompany me." She fell silent, allowing Barnabas to ponder the import of her earnest words.

Every instinct in him rebelled. If there was danger to loved ones, was he to sit in the lodges of the Arapaho? If LeBlanc was the source of those dangers, then wasn't he, as the man who had failed to kill LeBlanc, the one to stop him now? Was the elder, Sharp Nose, dreaming of one last military honor, to take responsibility for the accomplishment of Barnabas's mission and for the safety of Singing Grass? And was Squando, the Abenaki Prophet, forever to appoint himself the guardian of his friend's life? He felt the eyes of Singing Grass upon him, heard her unspoken plea to trust to Squando's advice and to believe in her to deliver kegs of powder in country she had traveled since earliest childhood.

"What a mess I made for all these people," he thought bitterly, "and I'm to watch while they clean it up. I'm damned if I do!" Yet, a voice, Squando's no doubt, whispered caution in his ear. "Think hard," it said.

"I will talk to Juniper," he said to Singing Grass, and she rose and left for her tipi relieved.

When Juniper returned, happily announcing that her three young horses were spoken for, he hesitated to speak. "Must I spoil her pleasure?" he thought. He decided he must. She had borne with his black moods long enough. It was past time to allow her back into his confidence.

She heard him out, asked no questions, made no interruptions. When the silence between them was sufficient to let her know he had finished, she spoke in the gentling voice her horses heard. She sensed him calming.

In the morning, Singing Grass, under the protection of Sharp Nose and leading two laden packhorses, left the village. Sky Feather had promised to keep the boys under her eye until they all reunited at the summer grounds. Juniper paced about in a quandary. When the little party of two had dwindled to spots on the horizon, Barnabas conceded and said to his wife, "Go."

Juniper flew to her horses, mounting her favorite paint and leading another. Sky Feather hastened to pack her mother's traveling needs with provisions that seemed to be already at hand. When Juniper paused to make her farewells, Barnabas handed a sack up to her. She knew by its weight what it contained. "Thank you, Husband, I will bring your pistol home to you," and she urged her horses into a gallop.

TEN

LeBLANC'S GOLD

LeBlanc was suspicious. From the beginning, there had been nothing but delay and disaster. He suspected Ruiz of leading them far astray. His speculations led him back to the merchant Ramon Flores in Santa Fe. That suave man had been in league with Ruiz, and Ruiz with the half-breed scout, Dominguez. His suspicions broadened to include Captain Rocher, who inspired no loyalty from his men.

LeBlanc had never been committed to the recovery of the hoard of gold. He felt no loyalty to Directeur Paul Barras or to the new French Republic. At heart, he remained a royalist. Even as the gold was being mined, he had siphoned off ingots and, with the connivance of a few confederates, now all bleached bones on the plains, had salted those ingots away in his own cache. He knew the spot by the triangulation of three distinct and towering peaks seen from a vantage point on a narrow pass. Marks he had chiseled into prominent rocks would lead him to his hidden hoard. He thought of that gold as rightfully his.

Dominguez reported directly to Ruiz. Ruiz then communicated to Rocher and LeBlanc their route as it lay ahead. LeBlanc had made it his practice to be within eyesight, if not earshot, when Dominguez made his reports to Ruiz. They were in the heart of sharply pointed mountains, like needles against the sky, by which he recognized that they must be close to the rich gold deposit, as well as to the scene of the massacre. His observation eventually provided him with the news he expected.

He watched intently as Dominguez conveyed with his hands the shape of a triangle pierced with an arrow pointing directly east over the ripple indicating a watercourse. LeBlanc knew that symbol; he had carved it himself. Dominguez must have stood, as he had stood, facing a prominent sandstone rock on the narrow pass below the three peaks. He knew the spot and that it dropped to a narrow, fast-running river, widening at a shallow crossing.

In the morning, after a night of scheming, he insisted that he accompany Dominguez on that day's reconnaissance. "I am familiar with this terrain. My eyes will see what memory has stored for me," he said. Ruiz was doubtful but had no logical objection to make. Captain Rocher was indifferent. Dominguez obligingly said, "Good to have two more eyes."

LeBlanc made a strategic decision concerning this half-caste. "Murder," he thought, "is not without consequences, but sometimes imperative. This man has served my purpose. He has led me to where I need to be. He must not lead anyone else there." LeBlanc did not spare a thought for the young French lieutenant he had smothered in his sleep at the old fort.

They rode for several hours. When finally they faced the mark on the stone, the scout said, "Too fresh to be Ute or Spanish. Your miners came this way. And we go where the arrow points." Those words hardened LeBlanc's resolve.

As they dropped down the trail, LeBlanc fell behind. At the river crossing, LeBlanc pulled from its saddle holster one of his two dragoon pistols, raised and sighted it down its twelve-inch barrel, and shot Dominguez squarely in the back. The scout slumped forward, and LeBlanc forced his horse close enough for him to push the man off his saddle and into the current. He watched unmoved as the body of Dominguez was swept away.

He seized the reins of the scout's alarmed horse and tied him to an alder tree on the bank. When the horse had calmed, LeBlanc removed the saddle. Using his short sword pulled from its scabbard, he carefully picked loose the stitching around the buckle that held the cinch tight. He then submerged the saddle into the river, wiping it clean of any drops of blood that might give away his game. He rebuckled the loosened saddle onto the back of the scout's horse.

At the top of the narrow pass, he used his sword again to scrape away the sign carved in the soft rock and flung up dust against it. As he retraced his way, he rehearsed to his satisfaction the sudden and tragic death of the scout, who was testing the river crossing before him. "His saddle suddenly slipped beneath the horse's belly, and Dominguez was flung against a rock in the river. By the time I got to the horse, the man was gone." The words came easily.

When the jingle of mounted horsemen alerted him that the column approached, he rode forward quickly and assumed a distressed expression. He told his story with appropriate regrets and self-recrimination that he had not able to either save Dominguez or to retrieve his body. Ruiz was stunned. Rocher was angered at yet another disaster to befall his expedition, but thankful it was not one of his soldiers.

"The death of Dominguez is a great loss, but I am in familiar territory now. The gold fields lie on the flank of that peak to the east." LeBlanc flung his arm in that easterly direction. Rocher's mood immediately lightened. The mention of gold swiftly passed through the troops. With their destination within reach, no one but Ruiz bothered to notice the dusty scrape marks on the rock when it was passed.

When the column camped in the shadow of the easterly peak, Ruiz privately approached LeBlanc. He had looked at the saddle cinch and was unconvinced. Dominguez was too savvy a scout to allow his gear to become so dangerously worn. The leather bore signs of meddling. He recognized that Dominguez had discovered a trail marker and that it had been defaced. Yet how to prove his suspicions that LeBlanc had murdered their scout?

"I looked at that cinch. Someone had picked at the stitching." Ruiz did not mince words. "May I look at your short sword?"

LeBlanc responded with a sneer. "You have no proof of what you suspect. From this point forward, it is I who can lead the column to the gold fields. Dominguez is the handy scapegoat for all that has befallen this expedition. Why not accept that convenience? One less man is more gold for those who survive." His hand unconsciously brushed his scarred forehead.

It occurred to LeBlanc that he could distract Ruiz with the story of the first expedition, of which he was the sole survivor. He would suggest to him that he needed another man's effort to unearth and to pack all those roughly shaped ingots of gold into the leather-bottomed pack bags he had acquired. He would richly reward a willing accomplice.

"I was the historian, appointed to record the successes, and the failures, of an expedition that has disappeared from all records. Those miners were sent in secret and they died in secret. Are you not curious? I know that you are."

Ruiz recognized that he was outplayed. There would be no justice for the half-caste Dominguez. Yes, he was very curious about where this trail led and why yet another man had to die to keep it secret. Gold was the only reason. He made himself comfortable, his back against a tree, pulled out a twist of tobacco, and gestured for LeBlanc to begin.

"It was an honor to be sent with that expedition. I was chosen because I had the credentials and the contacts. Years of hard travel in this godforsaken country passed, but for a long while, our numbers and well-armed guards kept the natives pacified. They seemed content to keep us under observation at a distance. Then our mining experts discovered an almost pure and inexhaustible vein of gold." He pointed his finger at the eastern peak.

"We were mining into the night using lantern light. As fast as the miners picked and shoveled huge nuggets of gold, smelters refined them into ingots while others cut down trees to feed the fires, build the sluices, and shore up the tunnel shafts. We were black with grime, exhausted and exhilarated.

Then those stupid nine men accosted a band of Utes and made advances towards their women. A man well hidden survived. After that, the savages lay siege and picked off the unwary. As more Utes were summoned, the encounters became pitched battles. The savages shot waves of arrows into the air, finding targets among the hiding. Many had muskets and were good shots. No one was immune from sudden death. Our commandant ordered that the gold be buried in the shafts, and I was called upon to make the map of where the gold was hidden. When our numbers had dwindled to an insupportable level, we were ordered to abandon the gold and to fight our way east to the open plains. The young lieutenant with me carried the official map. I carried my own copy. I took the precaution long before the onslaught to mark my path back to my hidden cache of gold. Then everyone was dead."

"But you survived, LeBlanc," Ruiz said in a mocking tone. "I think you are a man with luck on his side."

"Oh, it was not so much luck. I had planned my own exit, just as I plan one now. Amid all that chaos, I had handpicked confederates diverting ingots, which I carried away. I was merely the man who scribbled into journals. No one took notice when I came and went."

Ruiz chewed on his tobacco, apparently mulling over LeBlanc's proposition. He was suggesting that he, Ruiz, play the smart hand and become the man's confederate. He could return to Santa Fe a rich man. Perhaps Isabella would look at him in a new light. Perhaps Ramon would take him on as a partner. With gold, he could substantially help to free New Mexico from Spanish oppression. He considered these possible outcomes. Of one thing, he was sure. There would be no gold in the mining fields. There would be Utes instead. If any gold was to be carried away from these mountains, it would be the gold LeBlanc claimed as his own. He could ensure that LeBlanc paid a price in gold for killing Dominguez.

"You will need mules, LeBlanc." It was not an acceptance, but his words implied complicity. LeBlanc could infer what he wanted to hear.

"Three, I think, and I have picked the strongest mules. One of them carries the bags I require and provisions—let's say enough for two men," LeBlanc said with barely concealed eagerness.

"I could create a distraction tonight while you take the mules. In the morning, I could accuse you of murdering Dominguez, which you did, and of slipping away to get to the gold fields first. You retrieve your cache and go south. I'll catch up with you before you get to Santa Fe, and don't imagine I won't. You will need me to smooth your way out of Santa Fe to New Orleans. As you have seen, the Spanish government keeps a sharp eye on foreigners. The Flores family will require a fee for their services, as do I." Ruiz was pleased with the plausibility of his newly hatched scheme.

LeBlanc made an appearance of considering Ruiz's plan. "It could work. I warn you not to trust Rocher. He doesn't trust you, I can tell you that." LeBlanc laughed to himself. Trust was something none of them placed in one another. He had no intention of returning to Santa Fe and putting himself into the rapacious hands of Ramon Flores. He would take his chances going due east to the river called the Arkansas. He had studied it on French maps, and it could carry his cargo to the Mississippi. It had been his plan from the beginning. Ruiz could think what he pleased.

ELEVEN

AT THE GOLD FIELDS

Squando looked down into the deep crevice at his feet with grim satisfaction. It seemed that Mother Earth had shaken it wider since he and Barnabas had first gazed into it and planned what they could do with enough gunpowder. Through the brave action of their wives, Barnabas had delivered that gunpowder. Other bands had brought what they could spare. Along with Buffalo Bones and the combative High Winds, the three of them had just finished strategically placing those kegs into the crevice. In turn, each had wiggled down the crevice, securely roped to a boulder above. Each keg had been lowered in a basket and tightly wedged into place. The lid of the topmost keg was broken open to expose the powder, and piles of dry, brittle sagebrush placed on top as tinder.

A distance below on the rock face, Squando could make out the outlines of a tunnel where the French had dug into the mountain to open the rich seam of gold. The opening had been blocked, and he suspected that inside lay a quantity of gold ingots.

Scouts were coming in from all points, some reporting that a column of heavily armed men were riding in military formation from the western passes. Growler's Cub had not yet reported at the rendezvous below the Long Falling Water. Squando did not tell Singing Grass, who had remained after waving goodbye to Juniper and Sharp Nose, of his belief that his visions of whirling winds and Growler's Cub were somehow intertwined. He wanted this business with the French soldiers done with so that he could go in search of his son and set his wife's mind at peace.

High Winds could claim credit if the plan worked and blame Squando if it did not. He would win acclaim if he successfully carried out his part in the plan. With excellent reason, Squando was recognized as a mediator between men in dispute. High Winds would be appeased, and, it could be hoped, would make truce with his old enemy, Barnabas Locke.

High Winds approached, shaking dirt from his clothes. "Killing them all would be better," he repeated, "and save the gunpowder for ourselves."

The Abenaki shrugged and said, "If they refuse our offer, you may yet have your way. But these are soldiers and will follow the orders of their commander. Make *him* see reason and the matter is concluded without more death on either side. I believe death awaits the French in another place."

High Winds humphed and stalked away.

* * *

At a low ford, the column crossed the river two by two, separating to form a single frontal line on the bank upstream and down. Perhaps a parade ground's length lay between the halted line and the desolate remains of the mine workings, the mouth of the tunnel blocked. The Frenchmen could see across that stony space low, hastily erected barriers made of log and stone. Skeletons of men crouched against them, seeking shelter from a hailstorm of arrows that had pierced their ribcages. Naked human bones bleached in the sun, many with their skulls bashed in. They lay like silent witnesses to the rage unleashed upon them from above. Living men looked upon the dead with horror and approached no closer.

Rocher was not unmoved by the grisly remains of fellow Frenchmen, but he was furious with Ruiz. He openly blamed him for the defection of LeBlanc, gone in the night with the missing mules. Yes, he had likely murdered Dominguez, but what of that? Ruiz was playing some game of his own. Rocher turned in his saddle to again confront him.

"I think that sneaking bastard is making off with gold at this moment. Maybe you think we

French are stupid, but *this* Frenchman," and he thumped his chest, "thinks you and LeBlanc are in league with each other." Ruiz recognized that Rocher had become his deadly enemy.

Amid the angry accusations, a strong voice politely hailed the column from far above, "Bonjour, Messieurs!" As one, the two quarreling men looked upwards. All the Frenchmen looked upwards where an impressive array of natives stood like a bronze army. They had materialized out of the rock along the ridge lines, armed with muskets and bows. One tall, muscular man stepped forth on an outcrop, like a pulpit, and repeated his French greeting, holding a hand high to signify he would speak.

"I am Squando, the Abenaki Prophet. I speak on behalf of the Nuche, the Ute people whose territory this is. Come no closer. You are trespassers. You will take no gold from these mountains. You may take your lives."

Squando pointed left to a group of warriors, who raised their bows skyward. With the drop of Squando's arm, they loosed their arrows. As they fell to earth, the arrows encircled one tall stone standing apart. It was a magnificent display of marksmanship. Then Squando pointed to his right and more warriors loosed their arrows into the sky, duplicating the feat around another boulder even closer to the French line. The threat was unmistakeable.

Rocher called up, his voice angry but controlled, "I am Captain Auguste Rocher. I represent the Directoire of the Republic of France. I have come to repatriate the bones of these fallen French heroes to their native soil." Rocher clutched at a weak straw, knowing his position was untenable.

Squando again raised his arm to signify he would speak, replying in French, "Captain Rocher, as you see, we hold the upper ground. We greatly outnumber you. There is no place to hide, no defense you can make, no retreat possible. Look behind you across the river. Yes, you see yet more Nuche warriors. I tell you to go home.

"To guarantee that you never come back, that there is nothing for you to return for, we show you why." Squando pointed across the mountain face to the lone man standing well above the tunnel entrance—High Winds holding a burning torch aloft. Again, Squando dropped his arm, and High Winds threw the torch into the crevice yawning at his feet and ran like a goat across the ridge top.

In his wake, the mountain rumbled. It belched. It threw up a burning cloud of dust from every crack and crevice. With a thunderous roar, the mountain's face fractured in a jagged line above the tunnel entrance, crumbled, and slid downwards, sending an avalanche of flying rock and choking debris to engulf the minefields below.

When the rockfall subsided and the dust cloud cleared, the polite voice floated down. "There, the bones of your fellow soldiers are buried. Say your Christian words, and go home."

* * *

Covered in dust, Rocher turned his horse, his column of men reforming behind him, each pair crossing the river with shocked eyes fixed straight ahead. In a final humiliation, each mounted Ute in full war regalia, each war pony and warrior wearing paint, counted coup by touching with war club, lance, or hand, a French soldier as he passed. Rocher's command was broken. Expectations of gold and riches were obliterated. Each man wanted only to return still inside his bones to France.

The column climbed up through the pass where LeBlanc had left his marker. When they descended to level ground out of sight of the Utes, Rocher turned his fury onto Ruiz.

"You, you, and you," he barked, pointing to the three soldiers closest. "Take that man Ruiz and bind his hands behind him. He is under arrest. You are his guards. I want him out of my sight." The three appointed guards escorted Ruiz, who protested vigorously when his arms were yanked behind his back, to the rear of the column, behind even the mules. Ruiz had no allies among these dispirited men.

The ragged column of French soldiers followed their own track through the mountains. Game was scarce and hunger gnawed. Only scraps were thrown to Ruiz at the evening camps, when his arms were briefly released. During the daylight trek across this unforgiving country, Ruiz was choked by dust; his eyes burned; and his throat was parched. He remained alert for any chink of opportunity in which to escape. The three guards, equally weary of the dust thrown up by the column ahead, decided to tie Ruiz's horse to the pack mule directly in front. Where the trail widened, they rode like outriders. No one suspected that a pair of watchful eyes tracked their progress.

Despite hunger, thirst, and the failing horses beneath them, Rocher gave no quarter. He moved the column forward at a brisk clip. He sacrificed one mule to keep his men fed and then another. Mules no longer had a better purpose to fulfill. The landscape flattened as they approached the mesa where they had emerged from the canyon below on the day the earth shook. The sky was bright and the sun beat down.

Rocher was more than ready to rid himself of the inconvenient Ruiz before they passed into Apache territory. There was the matter of the dead scout. If pressed, he could blame Ruiz for his death. Ruiz had witnessed his humiliation at the gold fields, and he could not be allowed to tell that tale. He was also a confederate of the missing LeBlanc. He designated this sunny morning to be the auspicious time to hold him accountable. He rode back through the column to inform Ruiz of his fate.

"When we camp, I am calling a military tribunal of one. Me. You were once a soldier. Now a traitor, guilty of sabotage among other offenses. Prepare yourself to die." Rocher wanted the satisfaction of Ruiz begging for mercy, but the Spaniard only jutted his jaw in disdain. Disappointed again, Rocher spun his horse about and rode back to the front of the column. Ruiz stared after him with his mind spinning.

Oddly, the earth seemed to spin with him. Under the hot midday sun, columns of dust rose into the air and danced across the flat mesa top. As they twirled, they grew in height, sucking up dirt and stones in their dance. Tied to the mule in front, Pronto beneath him skittered in alarm. The braying mule surged forward. The rope between them snapped. Soldiers had dismounted to control their horses, and in the melee, Ruiz seized his chance. He recognized the dust devils for the nuisances they were, lasting only minutes and doing little damage. "Now," he shouted as he kicked Pronto away from the column. He leaned forward, clinging tightly with his legs. His horsemanship had always been his secret pride.

As the dirt devils swirled away, Rocher saw his enemy escaping. To the men closest to him, he shouted, "Shoot him, shoot him!" He pointed a shaking hand. A volley of musket fire rang out, and one ball hit its mark. Men cheered as Ruiz slumped in the saddle and then fell to the ground.

Rocher put a brusque halt to the celebratory claims. "Mount your horses," he ordered, "Column forward." The column rode on in the wake of the dust devils, now subsiding into little imps. No one cared enough to look back.

TWELVE

FRIEND OR FOE

Ruiz stirred. His head pounded. He tried to reach up a hand to his forehead, but his hands were bound behind him. He became conscious of another, sharper pain along his shoulder blade. As he painfully turned over and lifted his throbbing head, he saw a pair of moccasins. "From one fire into another," he thought in resignation.

A young warrior stood looking thoughtfully down. The short-barreled musket in his hand pointed directly at him. His other hand held a knife.

"Señor, are you friend or foe?" the young man asked in Spanish.

The question seemed unanswerable. Ruiz could not know if this Ute was a friend. Ruiz had ridden with his foes. Did that make him the young man's foe? He would prefer to be his friend. A name swam into his befuddled mind, and he replied.

"I am a friend of Barnabas Locke, the White Arapaho Man." The face above him broke into a smile.

"Then you are a friend. I retrieved your horse hoping it would be my own." The youth leaned down and cut the leather strap that bound Ruiz's hands.

"Thank you for rescuing Pronto. He has a good heart."

Since hearing the jingle of mounted men echo within canyon walls, Growler's Cub had discreetly followed the French column. He had put his hands over the noses of He Bites and Surefoot as they stood in the shelter of pines. His horses had pricked their ears forward as the column of men straggled by. The Cub had noted the swarthy, lean man bound and riding at the very end of the column. "A Spaniard," he had thought, "by the shape of his hat." Now, he handed that hat back to the Spaniard.

He acknowledged the man as a friend on the flimsy evidence of a claimed acquaintance with his Uncle Barny. It was a strange coincidence, and he would keep his musket at half cock. His present duty was clear—to aid this injured man while he continued to track the French through Ute territory, especially as they entered into the sacred forbidden grounds as they appeared to be headed.

They exchanged names as the Cub assisted Ruiz into the shelter of the pines where three horses were tied. He settled the man, brought him water, and examined his wounds. Ruiz had been lucky. The fall from the horse had done more damage than the ball that had cleanly passed under his shoulder blade. With water from his gourd, the Cub washed the blood and dirt from Ruiz's wounds.

"I have medicine," he assured Ruiz. He searched out the tightly woven little basket. "This salve has great curative powers. I have used it myself and also my horses." He liberally applied the salve to the entrance and exit holes on Ruiz's shoulder before bandaging the wound with a length of cloth, none too clean, ripped from Ruiz's spare shirt. He cleaned and swabbed the gash on Ruiz's forehead before dabbing the salve over it. He looked with satisfaction at his work.

They spoke together in a mix of Spanish, French, and American. "My uncle was right," the Cub thought. "It is useful to have the languages of these white people." In turn, Ruiz was impressed by the civility and expertise of this youth.

As they rested that evening, the Cub asked Ruiz, "How is it you know my tío, Barnabas Locke, the White Arapaho Man? My father Squando, the great Abenaki Prophet, is his brother. They wear the same Arapaho warrior's tattoo," the Cub proudly boasted.

Ruiz spat out the last of a twist of tobacco before replying, "I fought in a battle with your tío against Comancheros. We were almost as young as you. Your tío was clever and brave."

Growler's Cub nodded. "I know this story. You were the courier who bayoneted the Comanchero twice your size." He lifted his musket and released the half cock.

Ruiz was determined to arrive in Santa Fe before the French column. Passing through the Apache lands without Dominguez, he would have to safeguard himself. He hoped also to alert Ramon Flores that LeBlanc was on the loose and most likely riding to the Arkansas River as it wound its way southeast to the Mississippi. He might yet be headed off and whatever gold his stolen mules carried be retrieved. The idea that LeBlanc would escape justice as a rich man infuriated him.

The Cub explained that he had been warned by his tío not to trespass too deeply into the land of the Ancient Ones. He would ride with Ruiz and part from him before he descended off the mesa top.

"Do you know of a great city built by the Ancient Ones?" Ruiz asked the Cub, a long-held curiosity rising in him. But the Cub replied only, "It is bad luck to discuss such things," and turned over in his blanket.

Hours before sunup, before the moon had faded, the Cub shook Ruiz awake. "To get ahead of them, we go now. We cross the mesa top to the western side while the ground is damp with dew and hooves will pass quietly." He had wakened when the soothing chorus of coyotes suddenly fell silent in the night. Something larger was on the hunt.

They had only the last of a rabbit to break their fast. Ruiz was stiff, sore, a little dizzy from hunger, and needed a boost from the Cub to mount Pronto. They traveled companionably by the last of the moonlight until they saw the flicker of fires in the distance. They made a wide berth of the French encampment and traveled across a land bridge to the opposite side of the mesa. They passed through scrub trees and paused at an overlook above a narrow canyon to watch the French camp come awake. As the rays of the rising sun behind them touched the lower reaches of the canyon, both men gasped.

Ruiz breathed deeply in and then expelled his breath. "It is true. Here is the City of Gold built by the Ancient Ones. The Conquistadores went in search of it. These are the legends of my childhood, and now I see it for myself."

The Cub was dismayed, not thrilled, by the discovery. He turned in warning to Ruiz and said, "This is forbidden. Men do not live to tell what they have seen here. We must part." But he made no move to go.

Spellbound, they looked intently westward at the scene of the camp rousing from sleep. They watched as the fires above the city were stamped out. They saw a few small figures, men with muskets slung over their shoulders, using ropes to climb down a narrow broken path from the mesa top. They saw them stop in amazement at the sight of the city and then, spurred by an ungovernable lust for gold, they separated, running through the sandstone buildings, some higher than a pine tree, searching and touching and taking and throwing things down. The Cub was appalled by their desecration of a sacred place.

"This is what white men do," he snarled in condemnation. He was not alone in his outrage. Something alive stirred among the stone buildings. Suddenly, those men mad for treasure were running for their lives. One man shouldered his musket and fired. They saw the puff of smoke. He threw down the weapon and ran for the narrow path. He did not get there. A creature, strikingly spotted with a long tail, and far bigger than the mountain lion that had ambushed Surefoot, stalked these men with ferocious intent.

Two desperate men, having fired their muskets at a target that shifted in the blink of an eye, were cornered with their backs to a wall. They fixed bayonets but their assailant outflanked them and dropped upon them from the wall above. Ruiz shuddered in horror, and the Cub turned away from the carnage. They were unwilling witnesses to an execution.

The soldiers on top of the mesa peered down into the ravine, alarmed by the screams of their comrades, but the city clinging to the cliff face below was hidden from them. They were filled with the dread of yet another enemy destroying them in this hellish place.

Ruiz pointed to a man waving a sword above his head. "That's Captain Rocher trying to order men to their deaths. It's what he does." No one obeyed. The French soldiers hastily mounted and rode, not as a troop but as each man for himself, towards the land bridge from the far side of the mesa top.

"Time for me to go," Ruiz said urgently. "You have been a friend when I most needed one. I will not forget." And he kicked Pronto into a gallop.

Growler's Cub watched the Spaniard dwindle into the distance. The Cub tucked himself and his two horses behind a dense blueberry thicket. When the column passed in disarray, the faster and fitter first, the mules clattering on behind, he moved thirty-two beads on his counting cord. He waited long enough to ensure there were no stragglers. He sincerely hoped that Ruiz would outrun the murderous Rocher.

Eager to be away, the Cub turned his horses onto the trail, finally bound for the rendezvous at the Long Falling Water. As he rode off the mesa and deep into the cool of the aspen forest, he pondered what and how much of what he had seen could be reported without breaking faith with the Ancient Ones. He felt the need of his father's counsel. He could report that he had last seen thirty-two demoralized Frenchmen riding out of Ute territory and likely into the arms of the Apache.

His mind had settled and he felt at peace when a galloping, unsaddled horse fell into line behind Surefoot. It was nondescript, reddish, plain, and lanky, unlike the horses ridden by the French. Then more horses and a few mules fell into line. The Cub recognized these mounts. It was strange beyond his comprehension, but these riderless horses had chosen him to follow.

THIRTEEN

THE SENTRY STONE

Ruiz dropped off the mesa onto a well-marked game trail. When he passed the cairn with the memorial stone for a horse named Henry, he knew he was on the right path. He wanted to fill his canteens and water Pronto before the survivors of Rocher's column arrived into the canyon.

Horse and man drank their fill. The canteens dripped with water. Pronto chomped on grass growing thickly around the spring. Ruiz sat back, hunting through his pockets for tobacco but finding none. Both of them needed a few minutes to rest. His gaze settled on the tall stone standing like a sentry on duty at the face of the rock shelter. He remembered that the earth shook—perhaps in anger—when the French soldiers attempted to scratch their names into that rock. He recalled Dominguez shouting in disgust and alarm.

"The Ancient Ones were here long before us," Ruiz thought, "and perhaps it is true that their spirit remains as guardians." As he fingered the cross hung around his neck, he vowed never to reveal the existence of either the Lost City or this private place with its mysterious symbols. He gave Pronto time for another few mouthfuls of grass and then mounted and rode down the canyon out of Ute Territory and into the high dry desert of the Jicarilla Apache.

* * *

Rocher had difficulty imposing any military discipline. These disappointed, angry men had little use for him. They were worn thin. They had no money to travel home. Their government would repudiate the official purpose of their presence. They would more likely spend time in Spanish gaols than in French houses of pleasure. As each soldier reached the pool of water, he pushed his horse's head aside to drink and fill his canteen. The soldiers squabbled among themselves for a place to kneel at the spring. The atmosphere was ripe for mutiny.

One soldier, having drunk his fill, pushed his way through the milling crowd of horses and men to stand below the sentry stone. It stood impassively, taller than himself, with a symbol, like a long coiled rope, etched into the red sandstone from top to bottom. He climbed the short slope, pulling his dagger from its sheath. He announced, loud enough for anyone to hear, that "no damn half-breed or officer for that matter" would keep him from leaving his mark in this hellhole. He pressed the dagger point into the center of the coiling rope, which seemed to vibrate before his eyes. When he tried to withdraw the dagger, the blade sank deeper into the stone. He cursed and tried again with the same result. It was unnatural, and suddenly he was terrified. Before his astonished eyes, the coil of rope swirled into circular motion. Where he had stabbed the stone, a dark hole opened and expanded. A shrill wind whistled from it. The soldier stepped back, fervently making the sign of the cross and uttering a chain of Hail Marys, drowned out by the intensifying whine of the whistling wind.

The men crowding around the spring spun about in disbelief. Horses broke free, bolting up and down the canyon. Soldiers covered their ears in pain. Rocher pulled his sword to command order, but the sword strangely flew from his hand, sucked into the funnel of wind issuing from the sentry stone. The stone exerted an irresistible, magnetic force crackling in the air. The funnel rose and grew, fed by what it inhaled. Shrieking men were powerless, incapacitated, pulled from their feet and consumed into the whirlwind. Contorted faces stared outward as though through thick glass and disappeared into the bottomless pit of the stone. Nothing escaped. Not a scrap of leather, not a boot, not a body. When the intruders had been swept away, like leaves in a high wind, the funnel collapsed into itself and the dark hole closed. The sentry stone again stood impassively. All that remained was the brass-hilted handle of a dagger, and then that fell to the ground and slid down the short slope.

FOURTEEN

CHEATING DEATH

LeBlanc cursed the balky mules. Handpicked for their strength, yet they protested the weight of the gold they carried and the forced pace. At last, he was in the forested foothills and, from his high vantage point, could see the plains stretching before him and the sweep of the river he sought. The mountains had oppressed him and now his spirits lifted. He had evaded pursuit. Ruiz, if he survived, had not caught up with him, nor any Utes. Almost as though he had jinxed his good luck, he suddenly heard hooves clattering against rocks and low human voices on the trail behind him. He was acutely aware that someone was reading the signs of his passage.

LeBlanc pulled one of his flanking dragoon pistols from its saddle holster, and stationed his horse firmly in the middle of the trail. It was not the persistent Ruiz or a band of armed Ute warriors. Unexpectedly, an old Indian man traveling with a woman appeared on the trail. A huge black dog trotted ahead and began barking ferociously. The mules tugged and shifted behind him. He raised the pistol in his hand and pointed it at the dog.

Sternly, the woman called, "Cuervo, Cuervo," and the dog reluctantly returned to her. She lifted an arm in what he recognized as a gesture of peace. He considered what threat an old man and a woman posed. They were witnesses; they would talk. It would require three shots to kill them all. He weighed which of the three would receive the first ball. The dragoon pistol was most accurate at this close range.

The woman called out to him in bad French, "We wish to pass. Put down your weapon." That an Indian woman accosted him in French decided him. He shifted the pistol from the dog to her.

Immediately, the old man uttered a piercing cry and launched his horse towards him. Bent close to his horse's neck, the warrior lowered the long, feathered lance he carried. LeBlanc was shocked by the old man's ferocity and even more by the deadliness of the long metal point of the lance leveled at him. Almost reflexively, he pulled the trigger of his pistol.

The warrior was almost upon LeBlanc when the lance fell from his hand. Slowly, smiling as he met Death, the old man dropped from his horse. Transfixed, LeBlanc was slow to recognize other dangers. Before he could withdraw his second pistol, the dog leaped upwards, snarling into his face and snapping at his throat. Together, they tumbled to the ground. The dog savaged LeBlanc's arm when the man lifted the spent pistol to club him.

At the woman's command, the dog reluctantly released LeBlanc's arm, a threat rumbling in his throat. At the woman's signal, he went in pursuit of the mules, kicking up their heels as they escaped off the trail. LeBlanc looked up into the implacable face of the Indian woman, mounted on her paint horse and aiming a pistol with deadly menace.

In a steady voice, she said in French, "You are LeBlanc. I know you by the scar my husband left on your face."

LeBlanc sighed in frustration. He would not allow that man or his wife or his dog defeat him. He moaned, cradling the injured arm in the other, and rose slowly to his feet with a great show of pain.

"Your husband sought to kill me. That old Indian tried to kill me. Even your dog tries to kill me," he sniveled, even as the good hand slipped up the sleeve of the injured arm and stealthily loosened a knife. He stepped abruptly to the front of the paint, who flung up his head. As Juniper swiftly turned in her saddle to keep him within pistol sight, he gripped her left knee, attempting to sink the blade into her thigh. She jerked her knee out of his grasp, but the blade opened a long gash in her flesh. When he raised the knife again, she pointed the pistol downward and shot it out of his hand. She raised the pistol to smash it against his head, but he grabbed her by the wounded leg and yanked her from the paint's back. As she lay stunned and bleeding almost beneath her horse's feet, LeBlanc lifted a rock to bash her to death. He was thwarted in yet another murder by the paint horse, who whipped his head about and viciously bit off half his ear. Staggered with pain, LeBlanc dropped the rock, slapping his good hand to his head to staunch the flow of blood. He had been bested in this battle against man, woman, and beast.

His horse ambled away down the trail and his gold-laden mules were out of sight with a dog chasing them. LeBlanc had no choice but to go in pursuit.

* * *

Barnabas tightened the cinch around Stands His Ground's belly. Against his wishes, Enoch was also saddling his horse to accompany him. He expected the return of his wife, Sharp Nose, his dog, and possibly Singing Grass within a few days. Barnabas felt an urgency to ride out to where his people would drop out of the mountains onto the plains. He calculated the likeliest place would be just above the marshlands where the Arkansas River spilled onto the plains.

Enoch had tired of village life. He had enjoyed the storytelling around evening campfires and Sky Feather's lively interpretation, assisted by her father. The Arapaho encouraged their guests to tell their stories of the Indian Wars to the east. News of that conflict had drifted west on the lips of traders. Had they seen the famed Blue Jacket, the Shawnee war chief who had led his united forces in valiant defeat at the Battle of Fallen Timbers? They asked probing questions of strategy and tactics, and Enoch gained new respect for their warrior society. But his mission was not to swap war stories or to hunt with Arapahos, but to salvage stolen gold. He knew in his bones that his cousin had concealed from him the story of that gold, and he didn't want him far out of his sight. Barnabas had enforced the compromise that the sergeants stay behind.

Although Sky Feather wanted to accompany her father, she knew her duty to the little boys, and she had friends among the Arapaho girls. She rode out with her father and her cousin for some miles, practicing her American. Sky Feather knew all about that gold and her family's role in making sure it never left the mountains, but she breathed not a word about it. She turned her pony back to the village with a sigh.

The cousins rode a full day closer to the mountains. They camped near a stream shaded with cottonwoods where people of the plains had congregated for generations. In the morning, Enoch finally broached the delicate subject of gold but in a roundabout way.

"I am curious what sent Juniper and Singing Grass off to the mountains with all that powder."

"Very simple, Cousin. To bring down a mountain on all that gold that everybody seems to want except the folks who own it. That's why, Enoch, I've been keeping you and the sergeants under a sort of house arrest. I figure you got orders to confiscate as much of that gold as you can. A dangerous enterprise. The Utes would show you, or me for that matter, no mercy. Better that we're all out of the way of what's Ute business." They rode for some while each thinking hard thoughts.

Enoch broke the silence with the comment, "I sure hate to report back to Ned empty-handed."

Barnabas felt a twinge of sympathy for his cousin. "I once told your brother that 'being dead is no adventure.' Being alive is better than dead. You can report with full truth that there is no gold to be had. And anyone who thinks different will end up dead."

They found other subjects to talk about. Enoch said, "When you tell Squando that his sister Molly is dead, tell him Zeke left Vermont, though it's a free state, for Canada. Up in Niagara, a community of black folks has taken root. Runaways seek sanctuary up there, and free blacks give them shelter and a fresh start. He wanted to give their boy, Moses, a home with a future. Zeke worked your farm hard and made a good living off it. He sold it back to us Lockes. Ned wouldn't have it any other way. So, he's got the wherewithal to make a good life for himself and Moses. Maybe find a wife, but none like Molly."

In good time, they came upon the Arkansas, spilling out of the mountains but slowing through marshlands spreading beyond its banks onto the plains. It was a good hunting place for beaver. Enoch was astonished by the size and height of those beaver lodges. They followed the river west into the foothills, Barnabas alert for any sign that a traveling party with a large dog and at least four horses had passed. He found no sign at all. He grew increasingly uneasy.

When a flock of cranes noisily announced their passage along the river route, Barnabas looked up and spied a feather falling, drifting in the breeze and into his upstretched hand. The hair on the back of his neck rose. He pushed Stands His Ground into a gallop and called over his shoulder to Enoch.

"We must move fast. Juniper needs me."

They were pounding up a grassy slope when a shot reverberated among the surrounding hills, echoed, moments later, by a second shot. They urged their horses faster.

A familiar bark resounded across the meadow, and Barnabas saw a thing surprising enough to make him bring Stands His Ground to a sliding halt. Enoch rode up beside him, and the cousins looked across the meadow together in shared amazement.

"Enoch," Barnabas said, "here is a strange sight. That's Cuervo leading three mules in a line. I lay odds those mules belong to the man who is riding hell-bent towards them. If those mules carry what I think they do, then that rider is LeBlanc. Kill that man, Enoch, and whatever is on those mules is yours to take. I must find Juniper." He touched the horsehair band on his arm. As the cousins parted ways, Barnabas turned his head to shout a warning.

"You will know LeBlanc by the scar I left on his forehead. Remember, he cheats Death." Too late, he remembered that the man carried a sword.

* * *

Enoch's intention was to head off LeBlanc, if that was the rider, before he reached the mules. Cuervo already had possession, but whether that gave Enoch a claim was up for debate. He felt the exhilaration of riding into combat, his military instincts revived after these long months of travel to arrive finally within sight of his mission.

He halted his horse a bare moment before LeBlanc, and the scar on that man's angry face made his identity clear. Cuervo knew him as his enemy, growling and his tail rigid with threat. Enoch ordered him, "Stay," and the dog dropped to his haunches, the lead strap to the mules dangling from his slobbering mouth.

"We meet again, Barnabas Locke. Your wife has tried to kill me, but she is the one lying in the dirt." LeBlanc was dripping blood, but he held the loaded mate of his pistol in his good hand.

Enoch realized that LeBlanc mistook him for his cousin. His boast about Juniper enraged him, but he maintained a steely resolve to kill this man at any cost. The length of a keelboat or so lay between them. Enoch raised the Springfield rifle lying across his lap.

"You are a dead man, LeBlanc," Enoch said in English and the man responded in the same language.

"What if I surrender, Barnabas Locke? Do you kill a wounded man?" LeBlanc spat contemptuously and threw the loaded pistol to the ground between them. He then dismounted, making a show of his injured arm and wiping his kerchief over his damaged ear. The man made a spectacle of defeat.

Enoch cautiously threw a leg over his horse's neck and slid to the ground in a fluid motion, with his rifle held steady. Not for a moment did he dismiss LeBlanc as disarmed. He needed to see him at closer range and examine what was stored on his saddle and in his saddle bags. He slowly walked his horse closer to the gun on the ground but did not risk the inattentive moment to pick it up. Instead, he kicked it further away.

"You are a taller man than I remember and maybe younger," LeBlanc said with honest curiosity.

"I am his cousin, Captain Enoch Locke of the United States Army," Enoch replied shortly. He did not like all this conversation with a man he was about to kill.

"An Army officer, you say. Then I surrender to the United States Government. I rely on your military honor, Captain Locke, and on your respect to a duly credentialed envoy of the French government." LeBlanc stalled for time. He, too, moved his horse closer, but with the horse angled away from Enoch's full view.

LeBlanc spoke calmly. "I am going to retrieve my credentials from my saddlebag for you to examine. You will remember that we stand on Spanish territory, Captain, so neither of us has a legitimate right to assassinate a foreign official without consequence."

Enoch was becoming exasperated. He wanted to get on with the business at hand, and this talkative man was delaying matters. He was sure that LeBlanc concealed a pistol in those saddlebags, not pointless papers.

"Just throw the saddlebags to me, LeBlanc, and be done with it," he ordered curtly as he moved within yards of the man he planned to kill.

With his uninjured arm, LeBlanc slowly and deliberately lifted the saddlebags, unstrapping and opening them. Instead of throwing them to Enoch's feet, he flung them hard and high to hit Enoch, or at least to throw him off balance. He seized the short sword he carried behind the saddle on the right, the view of the horse he had concealed from his enemy.

"Hah!" he shouted, closing the short distance between them with his sword thrust forward. Desperation made him quick, and he was instantly upon Enoch, the blade swinging towards his neck. Enoch took one hasty step back and parried the swing with his Springfield, his finger on the trigger. Upon the impact of the sword against the wooden stock, the rifle discharged into the air. Dropping the rifle with the precious shot lost, instinctively, Enoch reached to his hip for Ned's tomahawk. The balance of power had instantly shifted to hand weapons—a short sword wielded by a skilled but injured swordsman and a tomahawk, a weapon Enoch had never used in combat.

LeBlanc reacted the faster of the two. As he again closed quarters, swinging his sword closer to Enoch's exposed throat, Enoch stepped forward and mightily swung Ned's tomahawk against the blade, striking a spark and snapping the steel. LeBlanc was stunned as his sword spun in pieces from his good hand. His shocked eyes rose to Enoch's implacable face as Enoch stepped even closer and delivered a sharp left hook to his jaw that sent LeBlanc sprawling backwards onto the ground. But luck had not deserted him. He might yet cheat Death. His scrabbling fingers found his dragoon pistol lying beneath him. As Enoch surged towards his prone body, LeBlanc rolled over, cocking his pistol and raising it in a last attempt to shoot Enoch dead. As his good arm rose, the dog Cuervo's massive jaws engulfed his forearm. Even as LeBlanc screamed in pain and despair, Enoch brought down the tomahawk, splitting open LeBlanc's skull.

Enoch stooped, panting and dazed, a long moment over the man he had been ordered to kill. In his hand, Ned's tomahawk dripped human blood for the first time since it had been forged by an old Swede blacksmith.

Cuervo trotted back to the lead line he had dropped and continued up the meadow with his charges.

FIFTEEN

A WARRIOR'S NAME

Juniper was stoic. Barnabas was distraught. By his cousin's arrival, Barnabas knew that LeBlanc was finally dead, although his eyes narrowed at the bloody tomahawk in his cousin's belt. Cuervo kept the mules under his control.

"I need moss and the large leaves of the bush growing along the stream bed," she told Enoch, describing through Barnabas's translation what she needed. Enoch went in search. Barnabas pressed handfuls of grass against Juniper's wound, a serious, unsightly gash but not deep. She was highly annoyed by the long tear in her bloodstained buckskin travel dress. Both of them avoided for the time being the body of Sharp Nose, which Barnabas had respectfully moved into shade and covered with his saddle blanket.

"He was smiling when he died," he reported to Juniper.

"He was a great warrior to his last breath," she replied.

After Enoch returned with the moss and leaves that Juniper said "would do," and after she had applied the potent contents of a small woven container to her wound, she supervised its bandaging and pronounced herself ready to travel.

The cousins lifted with ceremonious care the frail body of the fallen Sharp Nose onto his horse, who willingly accepted the burden. Barnabas pointed out the fading circle tattoos on his chest and told Enoch some of the successful coups in battle and in horse-taking that the symbols signified. They lashed him upright and across his back fixed his long lance. The osage wood bore the patina of many years and was decorated with eagle feathers, another symbol of the high status Sharp Nose had earned.

The eagle feathers prompted Barnabas to remember the crane feather that had drifted as a signal into his hand. He had woven it into Stands His Ground's mane so as not to lose it as they galloped. When he presented it to Juniper, they smiled at one another in a fashion that made Enoch wonder what part of their story he would never know. A pair of blue eyes sprang into his mind.

When the cousins parted, the lead line to the mules was tied to Enoch's saddle. Cuervo relinquished it with reluctance. No mention whatsoever was made of gold.

"Crisp and McFee will join you where the confluence of rivers makes one mighty one, the

Arkansas. Follow that river eastward to the Mississippi. May God and good luck go with you, Cousin. If you encounter hostiles, speak the name of Squando, the Abenaki, and his reputation will safeguard you. Tell Cousin Ned I think of him and still miss his cheerful face."

They bid farewell and the parties separated on their own journeys.

Sharp Nose was the first to ride into the Arapaho village. His horse carried him straight to his lodge. Warriors of all ages crowded about to respectfully lower him into their waiting arms. The women gathered to bewail his death. The aged Blue Smoke was summoned to conduct the burial rites. Quietly, Barnabas instructed the two sergeants where to find their captain. Two Rivers sent a suitable youth of his kinship to escort them to the confluence, and the sergeants departed after making small gifts of thanks to their hosts.

Sky Feather put her strong young arms around her mother and helped her hobble into their tipi. The little boys, healthy and hearty, came running to offer assistance. Juniper's first words were praise that her daughter had cared well for her little cousins. "You are becoming a woman," she said with gratitude to the Creator in her heart.

* * *

Deep in the mountains to the west, Growler's Cub was turning over in his mind what name he would adopt as a warrior. Behind him, the lanky red horse led twenty more, and they had fallen by habit into two columns. Two mules followed. At night camp, the horses grazed freely yet came together in the morning behind the red horse to follow the Cub, Surefoot and He Bites. They formed a strange parade.

* * *

Squando and Singing Grass crested a hill and stopped to give their horses a breather. Mountain meadows stretched ahead, dotted with stands of aspen, cottonwood, and alder and crossed by little streams and sprawling ponds, each capped with the stick pyramid of a beaver lodge. Rich pickings for the booming fur trade. Squando rose in his Ute saddle.

"What do you see, Husband?" Singing Grass asked idly.

"I see our son riding towards us with many horses behind him," he replied.

She laughed at his jest and then her laughter turned into a cry of joy.

As the family reunited, the riderless horses broke ranks to graze. The Cub was eager to share his adventures but hesitated to speak of certain things. He turned to his father, his arbiter in all matters of manhood, to ask his advice.

"My uncle warned me not to travel too far onto the mesa where I was posted. Not to take anything. Not to speak of what I might see there." He looked to his father for affirmation.

"That is so. But these horses following you like dogs, can you tell us that story?" Squando waved his hand expansively over the scattered horses, thin and unkempt but not the ponies of the plains.

"A shabby red horse, not a stallion, not a fine-bred Spanish horse, a lanky little red horse led them to me. As though that horse saw me as his leader, and the rest fell in behind. I did not recognize the red horse, but I knew the rest as the mounts of the French soldiers." The Cub looked over the herd to spot and point out the little red horse. He was not there.

A remembrance of heaving an ancient Arapaho warrior onto the back of just such a horse flashed into Squando's mind. He looked thoughtful.

"You must ask Juniper about spirit horses. Also your uncle."

Later, judging his moment, Growler's Cub broached the matter of the name by which he was known. He knew that his father, Squando, had chosen that name for him as a tribute to the Bear Dance where he and Singing Grass had danced together. The Cub believed he merited a name worthy of a warrior, especially one who returned from a distant outpost with a herd of horses.

"Paints Horses, I think," the Cub proposed. His mother and father exchanged glances. "It is a good name. We will talk about it," Singing Grass replied. She was not yet ready to relinquish her cub.

EPILOGUE

"Walk beside me so we may be as one."
—Ute saying.

MESSENGERS arrived bearing letters to Barnabas Locke, the White Arapaho Man. Each lifted his restless spirits for a short time. The first came from Santa Fe, much as the one sent a year ago, but this time delivered by the reliable Arapaho youth who was a kinsman of Two Rivers. The letter was again from Ramon Flores. No gift was included. It read, in part:

> *Ruiz returned in rough shape but alive. None of the Frenchmen he guided returned. Nor did the scout Dominguez. This created trouble with the authorities, but Ruiz has been exonerated. He spoke highly of a young Ute called Growling Cub (if he got that right). The young man saved his life and he prays he returned safely.*

The second letter arrived in late summer the following year. It came from St. Louis, first carried by Charley Potatoes who handed it off to a Cheyenne, a trader in buffalo hides, when they had greeted each other at the Osage watering hole. The Cheyenne, in turn, put the letter into the hands of Two Rivers when collecting hides from the summer hunt. Two Rivers entrusted it to the same youth, now grown, who had delivered the letter from Santa Fe the previous year. The stiff envelope, much smudged, bore a wax seal stamped with the names "Jones & Locke." Barnabas fingered those words with a smile. When he broke the seal, two pages of good paper were folded together inside. The briefer one read:

> *Received hides and beaver pelts in full payment*
> *of outstanding account. My name on the business*
> *is a powerful asset and I intend to keep my hand*
> *in. Your cousin, I think, is the right fit. He has*
> *accepted the same offer I once made you, but he*
> *was smart enough to take it. Inclosed see personal*
> *letter writ by him. Trust you and family are in*
> *good health.*
>
> > *Regards, Joshua Jones, Esq.*
> > *Land Agent & Merchant*

The longer letter was written closely on both sides, with a postscript in a feminine hand. Barnabas read it twice over, once slowly and silently to himself and then aloud in Ute to Juniper. After long discussions, they came to an agreement. Only then, did Barnabas hand the second letter to Sky

Feather and assisted her in reading it as her reading vocabulary did not match her verbal command of the language. It read in part:

Cousin, I inquired, as your daughter asked I do, whether St. Louis has a school for girls where she would be welcome. There is a fee school at the Catholic Church, and I have talked with Mother Superior Benedictus. Mr. Jones has been persuasive, as only he can be, in making the arrangements. My wife and I will gladly serve as her guardians. We very much want Sky Feather to stay with us in our home while she completes her education. Should these arrangements be acceptable to you and your wife and daughter, we will provide necessary clothing, school supplies, etcetera.

Here followed the details of the financial arrangement, as well as the list of things Sky Feather would require. The letter writer resumed:

My wife is excited about the prospect of Miss Sky in the house. My Daisy is a levelheaded but high-spirited young woman herself. Now for matters of recent business. Ned is thankful for what you were able to do for certain parties. Not even a handful of officials know the circumstances of this windfall, and none, not even

*Ned, knows the full story. I have been assured
that no record in any ledger was ever made.
Daisy and I did not cotton to life in the District
(muddy noisy and treacherous) and I resigned my
commission. Your Mr. Jones made me an offer in
your part of the world I could not refuse.*

Enoch continued with more family news, but
it was the message from Marguerite Locke, once
known as Daisy Bellevue, addressing Juniper that
most interested Barnabas's family.

*"Juniper, you are much in my thoughts. Sky
Feather will be like a little sister to Enoch and
me so long as she chuses to stay. Your husband
will not remember me, but I remember him.
I was a small girl sitting on the porch at the
trading post in Kittanning when he rode there
on business. I was one of the children rescued by
Simon Girty and left in their care until we were
claimed. I never was. The Bellevues kept me as
their daughter. We share bonds of friendship."*

Juniper wrestled with her headstrong daughter's desire to go east and learn American ways. At
the Bear Dance, the girl had flicked her shawl at
many suitors. Several offered generous bride prices,
but Sky Feather had smiled and refused them all.
Singing Grass was privately disappointed that

Sky Feather and Paints Horses were content to remain brother and sister. Barnabas felt pride in his daughter's independence. Squando wisely made no comment.

When Barnabas and Juniper returned from St. Louis, leaving their beloved daughter to embark on her great adventure, Barnabas sank into low spirits. Juniper sought advice in a quiet moment alone with Singing Grass. "He looks to the west. When he speaks, and he speaks little, he speaks of the great mountains and riverways to the west. He yearns to see the great waters his people call the Pacific. He waits for me to say what is in his heart."

Singing Grass thought the matter over and at the right moment consulted with her husband, who was, after all, the one who knew best the secret heart of his lifelong friend.

Singing Grass reported Squando's advice to Juniper. "Let him go or go with him." Juniper had come to the same conclusion—that her husband was not a proud horse to be gently broken to her will.

"What is there to keep him from going west? What beckons him always west? Will he return? Would I know if he was dead? Should I go with him?" These were questions she asked of herself and then privately to Singing Grass and eventually to the White Arapaho Man himself.

"I am still fit and strong. I would like to see that great ocean that lies to the west. I can go no more west than that. I will come back to you with shells from its shores. I will walk beside you again." Barnabas said this to Juniper in halting words. He struggled to explain even to himself the tug and pull of the west on his spirit. It had ever been so.

With those words, Juniper saw that her husband yearned for a journey in which she played no part. She smiled into his troubled face and said the words he needed to hear. "Then it is settled. Mother Earth will welcome you on the trails you follow into the west. Stands His Ground is ready for such a trial and Tries Hard has proven himself."

* * *

Squando rode his plain brown horse some miles west with his friend. They rode in companionable silence as all the words had already been said. Barnabas broke the silence as he mused aloud on something that had long intrigued him.

"I heard that the Paiutes talk around their campfires about an enemy people of red-haired giants, taller than even the Osages. What do you make of that?"

Squando snorted. "Don't get yourself eaten." With a salute of farewell, he turned his brown horse and galloped east.

Startled, Barnabas looked after his departing friend. "Eaten?" he wondered. "Has Squando seen another vision about me?"

About the Author

MATTHEW BLAINE enjoys swapping tales with interesting people with their own stories to tell, especially around a campfire. Although his education was hampered by dyslexia, he found another sort of education in the company of Ernest Hemingway, Jack London, Louis L'Amour, John Steinbeck and outdoors adventure magazines. After stints as a cab driver, steelworker, factory floor assembler, and carpenter, he worked for thirty years managing trade shows on the East Coast. During the pandemic, he wrote two self-printed memoirs about his travel and outdoor adventures. That triggered an ambition to write honest fiction in which he could reinvent himself in the lives of historical characters. An avid primitive archer, canoeist, long-distance hiker, minimalist, and unionist, Matthew enjoys delving into obscure stories of the past.

Retired, he lives in rural Pennsylvania, haunting flea markets for goods to trade with fellow outdoorsmen at swaps and archery rendezvous. In a shop inside his woods, he practices the skills required for leather working, shaping and fletching primitive arrows, and marrying old axeheads to newly-fashioned handles.